A Heartless Goon
Snatched My Soul

Nika Michelle

Cover design by Bryant Sparks

Chapter 1

Atlanta

2017

Running into him again made all those old memories come crashing back in like ocean waves during a tsunami.

"Xavia, is that you?" Staring at me in shock, he knew exactly who I was, but it had been five years since we'd seen each other.

He was rocking the same close haircut, and his dark, coffee skin tone was still as smooth as ever. The full beard he'd grown out was the only thing that was different. Mmm, he was still fine with those cognac colored, bedroom eyes.

"Who do you think it is... Eddie?" Rolling my own honey brown eyes at him, I walked off to go inside and pay for my gas.

He was the first man I'd ever loved, being that I had never met my father. The explanation my mother gave for his absence was, he wasn't ready, or willing to be a father, so I didn't need to know who he was. According to her, he wanted her to abort me, which made me hate a man I didn't even know. My childhood was hard as hell and in a world full of evil, Eddie had become my savior. I wasn't raised in church and didn't know who God was, so that was Eddie to me. By the time I was six years old, my mother was a full-fledged alcoholic and so was her husband.

He often pimped her out to support his cocaine habit. Sometimes her johns would come to our house when her husband was there. He'd sit right on the sofa in the living room as if nothing was going on. After two years or so, he left my mom and she decided to prostitute on her own. Not only did she neglect me in every way, but by the time I was eleven, she decided she wanted to pimp *me* out.

Just like it was yesterday, that shit lingered in my memory. Some tall, lanky, light skinned man with ugly features just busted in my bedroom late one night. As his wide nostrils flared, he stared down at me while I laid down on my bed. My nightgown clung to my sweaty body because it was the middle of June and we didn't have an air conditioner. My window was up, but the stale, warm air wasn't helping to cool me off at all.

"Mmm... you one pretty lil' bitch." The strange man rubbed his hands together and licked his, dry, cracked, chapped lips.

His musty smell permeated throughout the room as if he hadn't bathed in years, if ever. I'd never seen a man's penis before and when he pulled it out the stench in the room got worse. Was that what a man was supposed to smell like? My mother's ex-husband had a foul body odor too. Eww, I felt so nauseas and the bile threatened to come up as I dry heaved.

"What you doin' in my room?" My young, slim frame trembled as I asked.

"Don't ask me no questions you lil' bitch," he growled grabbing me by my ankles.

"Mommy…. Arrgghhh! Mommy!" I screamed out as he pulled me toward the edge of the bed.

Placing his funky hand over my mouth, he yelled. "Shut the fuck up!" His hands spread my thighs and roughly reached for my panties. "That bitch don't give a shit 'bout yo' ass."

Kicking and screaming, I fought back with everything in me.

"I already paid yo' mama for this pussy, so you better keep still before I…"

That's when my foot connected with his face and then with the other foot, I kicked him in the balls. As he held on to his nasty dick, I bolted through the opened window. Without even thinking about it, I knocked on Eddie's bedroom window. He spotted me and opened it quickly. Glancing up, he saw the silhouette of the pedophile in my room.

"Did he hurt you?" His eyes filled with concern as he let me in.

"Almost." I sniffled and wiped away my tears. "Can… can I stay here? I'll sneak out in the morning so yo' mama won't see me."

Eddie was two years older than me and his sister Alicia was my best friend. If she wasn't away for the summer in Alabama with her grandmother, I would've knocked on her window. When my mother's tricks would come over after that, it became a ritual for me to climb out of my window and knock on Eddie's. He'd always let me sleep in his bed while he slept on a pallet on the floor.

During that summer, Eddie and I grew closer. Although his sister was my best friend, my bond with him ended up turning into something deeper. By the time I was thirteen, my feelings for Eddie grew into something more. With hormones raging, I lost my virginity to him. I'd snuck into his bedroom plenty of times for security, so it was bound to happen.

The thing was, I didn't have too many friends other than Eddie and Alicia; well, except for this chick named Chloe. Most of the kids we went to school with, and in the neighborhood, picked on me because of who my mother was. They'd call her all types of sluts and whores, and so that made me a whore too. My mama didn't give a shit about me, so I often went without. Alicia always took up for me and everybody was afraid of her. She was a thick girl, with pretty, caramel brown eyes and mocha toned skin who would throw hands real quick. When it came to clothes, I didn't have the best. Most of the time I'd wear Chloe's clothes, or Alicia's mother would shop for me when she shopped for her children. I was grateful for that.

By the time I was sixteen, my mother literally left me on my own. One day, she just disappeared and soon the landlord put a padlock on the front door while I was at school. Alicia and Eddie's mother Margie took me in and I ended up graduating from high school the next year. Well, Margie made me promise that I'd finish despite what I'd been through with my mother. I had no idea where she was. I'd heard rumors that she'd moved in with some older man.

Margie knew about me and Eddie's relationship, but didn't allow us to sleep together. Sharing a room with Alicia didn't stop me from sneaking into Eddie's room. I'd become a pro at that. Something told me that she knew, but turned a blind eye. My birth control prescription was always filled and out of respect for Margie, I made her son use condoms. We'd slipped up a few times, but I wasn't dumb enough to bring a baby into the house of the woman who took me in when she didn't have to.

Eddie and I were really starting to get serious. He'd even asked me to marry him down on one knee and all. We had gone to the Cheesecake Factory in Buckhead for dinner and he proposed in front of everybody. As they clapped, I cried.

"Xavia, babe, I love you more than any words I could ever say and I wanna spend the rest of my life with you. Will you marry me?" His anxious eyes were peering up at me waiting for my response.

"Yes, yes," was my answer with no hesitation.

The rest of the night was the shit. We ate good and then got a nice room at the W Hotel. After making hot, passionate love all night, I just knew my life was going to change and all the bad shit was over.

Shit, I was wrong as hell. Eddie wasn't faithful to me at all, but I had no real proof. All I had were the rumors and my gut feeling. Those bitches wanted to fuck him so bad, they wouldn't tell me shit. Yeah, you could say he had his hoes in check. He was a street nigga who sold coke, weed and pills. Although he wasn't on kingpin type of status, he had deep pockets and ambition to run the drug game. The thing was, Eddie spoiled me with money and gifts. That only made me turn a blind eye, because I wasn't used to anybody taking care of me. In my mind, he loved me regardless of his so-called side bitches.

After two months of being engaged, I heard about him cheating on me again, but I ignored all the hearsay. Even Alicia made excuses for her brother.

"Girl, them bitches just hatin' 'cause you got Eddie and they don't," she'd always say.

One night, we went out because it was like I just needed to go somewhere and have a good time. Eddie was always out and about doing him, so why shouldn't I be out doing me? He claimed he was saving up for us to get our own place, but we were still in his mom's house. That nigga loved to spend money on bullshit like clothes, J's, video games and weed. Eddie had dropped out of high school in the eleventh grade. His mother didn't hold him up to the same standards as me and

Alicia, because she depended on his illegal money to get by.

Chloe didn't go out with us because she said she had a headache, so it was just me and Alicia. Her boyfriend Jermaine kept blowing up her cell phone and for some reason, I just wasn't enjoying myself. The entire time we were at the club, I had a weird feeling and I couldn't figure out why.

"Why don't we just go? I mean, it's lame as fuck in here anyway," I complained.

The club wasn't even packed, and Alicia didn't seem bothered by Jermaine calling her back to back.

"It ain't even one yet Xa."

"Well, I'm ready to go anyway." I'd just turned eighteen and had been looking forward to getting in the club legally, but I wasn't feeling it.

After calling Eddie's cell phone three times, I realized he wasn't going to answer. That made me want to leave even more, so, we left. The first thing I noticed when we pulled up on the street was Chloe's baby blue VW Bug. It was a cute car that we would all cruise around in. Alicia was driving her mother's white Honda Accord. Of course, I had no car. Eddie kept promising to buy me one, but I usually drove his.

"What the fuck's Chloe doin' over here?" Although it was a thought, I said it out loud.

Alicia shrugged her shoulders. "I'on know. She's parked in front of Jay's. Maybe she's over there smokin'."

Sucking my teeth, I shook my head. "But the hoe couldn't go out wit' us 'cause her head was hurtin'. That bitch is probably gettin' some dick. You think she fuckin' Jay?"

"She ain't said nothing, but he is fine though."

"True," I agreed. "He just too damn light bright for my taste."

We both laughed as Alicia pulled into the driveway. We got out of the car and walked inside.

"Girl, I'm 'bout to jump in the shower before Maine gets here." Rolling her eyes, she walked off to her bedroom.

Shaking my head, I headed to the bedroom that I shared with Eddie. Their mom must've been in bed already. Now that I was eighteen and we were engaged, she didn't care if I slept in Eddie's room with him. As I turned the doorknob, I thought about how I couldn't be with a dude like Jermaine. He was so damn jealous and controlling of Alicia. Maybe it was because of all that ass she was dragging back there. The thought made me laugh.

Eddie was like a normal type of jealous, and he didn't try to control every move I made. When I opened the door, and turned the light on, my eyes drifted toward the bed. They had to be deceiving me.

"Oh... hell nah!" My scream was so loud that Eddie literally jumped his butt naked ass up from the bed. His long, thick dick swung, and I noticed that he was wearing a condom, but that shit didn't matter.

"Baby, shit, what you doin' back already?" As he asked, he hopped up and down trying to get his boxers on in a haste.

All I saw was that bitch who I called my friend trying to grab her clothes and escape. "You ain't goin' no damn where bitch!" Grabbing her by her hair, I spun her around and busted her in the mouth hard as hell.

That bitch's lip split beneath my knuckles and I saw the blood gushing. Her teeth cut into my skin, but I didn't feel that shit at all. As I pulled back to swing again, I felt Eddie grab me. Then I heard Alicia's voice.

"What the fuck's goin' on in here?" She asked just as I heard Margie walking up.

"Oh shit... Eddie..." Margie shook her head not needing to ask what happened. "Get outta here now Chloe before I make him let her go, so she can beat yo' triflin' ass!"

"You better be glad my mama's standin' here bitch, or I'll finish that ass whoopin' for Xa." Alicia was fuming. "The fuck kinda friend are you?"

Chloe scurried toward the front door in just her underwear. I guess the bitch planned to get dressed in the car with her trifling ass. Yeah, she was a slut bucket, but I never thought she'd do that shit to me.

"Fuck!" Eddie shook his head knowing that all hell was about to break loose on his ass.

"It's bad enough you did that shit. How you gon' do that shit here where yo' girl lay her head?" Shaking her head, Alicia walked off. "I can't wit' this nigga."

"Boy, I wanna go upside yo' head right now, but I'll let y'all talk first. You gon' have to deal wit' me later Eddie." Margie sighed and turned to leave the room. "Just like yo' sorry ass daddy."

"Talk? I doubt it's gonna be any talking goin' on. I wanna hurt this mufucka! For real."

Margie simply shook her head and closed the door behind her.

Eddie's grasp hadn't loosened on my wrist. "Calm the fuck down..."

"Calm down? Are you for real? I thought that hoe was at Jay's, but she was here fuckin' you! How long you been fuckin' my damn friend and of all bitches, why her?" Man, I was so hurt that I couldn't feel.

Eddie held on to me, not loosening his grip at all. "That don't matter baby. Now you know that bitch ain't yo' friend," he said nonchalantly.

With my free hand, I did what his mother wanted to do. As I slapped him upside his head over and over, he attempted to block the licks.

"You fuck boy ass nigga! You know you and yo' family are all I got and you pull some shit like that! The only reason I busted that hoe's grill up and not yours was because I was savin' yo' ass whoopin' for later! Talkin' 'bout now I know she ain't my friend! Nigga, you ain't my man! Get yo' hands off me 'fore I kill you!" There was so much rage inside of me that I could feel it coursing through my veins.

"I'll let you go if you stop fuckin' hittin' me!" His eyes showed that those fiery smacks I was throwing were making him mad.

"You think I give a fuck 'bout you bein' mad nigga? Do you? Because I give zero fucks about how you feel right now!" The numbness I felt when I first saw that bitch riding my man had been replaced by a wave of emotions. I'd gone from being angry, to feeling hurt and betrayed.

Now the tears were dripping down my cheeks and making a wet spot on my black shirt. Suddenly I *really* wanted to hurt him, and I looked around the room for a weapon. There his revolver was laying on the dresser. As I reached for it, he lunged for me.

We struggled with the gun and I tried my best to get that shit from his ass. Shooting his damn dick off was my driving force. A bitch was on a mission to make sure that shit didn't work anymore.

"Let that shit go shawty. You ain't thinkin' straight baby. Don't do nothin' stupid. I'on give a fuck about Chloe. I don't want that bitch! You know she's a fuckin' hoe and you know I love you. Whose finger did I put that ring on? Who I put my dick in don't matter."

"Do you hear yourself nigga? You sound fuckin' stupid as hell. So, you had to fuck her too, huh? You might not give a fuck about her, but she *was* supposed to be my friend! Why'd you have to fuck that bitch! I fuckin' hate yo' ass!"

POW!

The sound of the shot made me remove my hand from the gun. It hit the floor with a loud thud and Eddie's eyes widened as he looked at me. Then my eyes drifted down and saw the blood leaking from his side.

"Oh shit... Eddie... shit... I didn't mean to..." By instinct I reached out and pressed my hands against the wound, putting pressure on it.

In no time Alicia and Margie were rushing in. It felt like the room was spinning as I tried to explain that the gun went off in a struggle and I didn't shoot him on purpose. Margie shook her head as Alicia called 911.

"I'm so... sorry..." What I was feeling then was guilt, but I was still hurting inside from what Eddie had done to me.

"I shouldn't have left y'all alone," Margie admitted. "I didn't think you'd..."

"It's okay... It's not that bad. It's just a flesh wound. I don't need no ambulance," Eddie spat through clenched teeth.

"I'on give a fuck what you say. You goin' to the hospital just in case," Margie snapped.

"Am I goin' to jail?" My voice was low and meek. Damn, I'd overreacted by trying to grab that gun.

"You better hope my son don't die Xa. I mean, you're like my daughter, but..."

"I told you it ain't that bad ma."

"I wasn't tryna shoot him. I was just in my feelings. You know I caught him fuckin' Chloe. I went to grab the gun, but..."

"Guns ain't nothing to play wit' baby girl." Margie shook her head and went back to attending to her son. "I didn't think you had that in you Xa."

"I told you already Margie. The gun went off when he tried to keep me from gettin' it. I didn't shoot him," I tried to defend myself.

Margie didn't say another word to me.

The ambulance came a few minutes later and I stayed back at the house. Wringing my hands together nervously, I waited for some news on Eddie. As much as I hated him, I didn't want him to die. I also didn't want to go to jail for murder. Fuck, what if Margie and Alicia turned on me? I mean, I wasn't their blood, Eddie was.

"He's okay. He was right. It was just a flesh wound. We explained it off as an accident," Alicia told me over the phone.

As much as I didn't want to return to that bedroom, I did. That was when I saw the bullet on the floor. It had made a clean exit through his skin and hadn't hit anything major. Still, I was furious at him for breaking my heart into pieces. There was no way I'd be the same again. The way I felt, there was actually a hollow spot in my chest. It felt like nothing existed behind my rib cage other than my lungs. For a moment, they didn't even feel like they were functioning. It was like I was suffocating in my pain.

Grabbing a suitcase that was in the downstairs closet, I put it on the bed and threw my meager belongings inside. Shit, I didn't have much. I'd already called my cousin Rosita who lived in Miami. She was nineteen and her mother, my aunt Barbara, was cool as hell. At one point she'd offered for me to come live with her, but I didn't want to leave Eddie's sorry ass.

Removing the engagement ring from my finger, I wondered how much I could get for it at a pawn shop. Only having a little over a hundred dollars to my name, I found Eddie's stash and grabbed a few hundred-dollar bills. That would buy me a bus ticket and some food as well as leave me a small cushion. Too bad I didn't know where he kept his real money.

After I called a taxi, I was out of there before they all returned home. Not giving a damn how long I had to wait at the Greyhound station, I just wanted to get away from there. No way in hell could I stay and look at the man who had not been loyal to me the same way I'd been to him. If I felt like shooting him before, who knew when that feeling would come over me again. The love I felt for him hadn't gone anywhere, although I also hated him. It was like I was on a rollercoaster ride of mixed feelings. There was truly a thin line between love and hate.

Seeing him all those years later only reminded me that I was still angry. At the age of twenty-three, I wasn't over it yet. As much as I thought I was, I realized that I wasn't. That feeling of fury was just as fresh now as it was back then, but somehow, I felt love for him too.

Chapter 2

Atlanta

2017

When I walked out of the store Eddie was waiting for me. As if he wasn't even there, I walked right past him.

"I'm so happy to see you Xa, for real."

The feeling was not mutual. Not saying shit, I headed toward my car and proceeded to pump my gas.

"So, why y'en say shit to nobody all these years? You could've at least talked to Alicia."

Ignoring him, I finished, opened my car door and got behind the wheel.

"You still mad shawty? That shit was *years* ago and you the one who almost killed me."

"And I see that you're still an arrogant son of a bitch." Turning the key in the ignition, I put my foot on the gas, but that fool stood in front of my car before I could pull off.

"Shit! Move Eddie! If you think I tried to kill you before, you ain't seen shit yet."

Letting out a chuckle, he clearly didn't think I'd run him over. In my mind I saw myself rolling over him and then backing up to roll over him again. The thought made me let out an evil cackle.

"See, you know you ain't gon' run me over." There was that cute smile I used to love. Oh, how I detested it now.

"Hmm, you just don't know that I was picturing that shit."

He snickered like I hadn't just told him I was thinking about running him over. "Look, I'll move if you just let me talk to you for a minute."

Shaking my head in annoyance, I took my foot off the gas and agreed just so he'd leave me alone. "A'ight, but I ain't got all day. I gotta make some runs before I head back to my mom's. I didn't come back here to see you. I'm just visitin' her for a few days."

"Oh, so you talkin' to your moms again?" Eddie walked back to my side of the car. "That's what's up."

"Yeah, a couple years ago she reached out to my aunt and found out I was in Florida."

My mother had finally gotten herself together and had a job as a cashier at Publix. She had also found real love and he'd helped on her road to sobriety. I was glad she was sober, but it had taken years for me to forgive her. Eddie wasn't so easy to forgive though.

With a nod, he said, "Cool. I'm actually glad you two are workin' on your relationship. She even went to my mom's lookin' for you. We ain't have no idea where you was."

"That was how I wanted it."

"Mmm, I get that and all, but why don't we work on our relationship too?" As he bit down on his bottom lip, I could feel that weakness for him creep back.

Giving him a blank stare, I asked, "And what relationship is that? Bye Eddie. This conversation is over."

"But Alicia and ma ain't do shit to deserve you not fuckin' wit' them, I did. Why take it out on them?"

Not wanting to talk about it, I still went ahead and gave him an answer. "Not that you deserve an explanation, or whatever you're looking for, but I didn't take shit out on them. It's just... well... to separate from you, I had to separate from them too. You wouldn't understand, and I don't expect you to. I just had to do what I had to do, and it was the best decision I've ever made. Now, I have to go."

"Well, I ain't done talkin'." His eyes bore into mine, searching, but there was nothing there for him to find.

"I am and this time if you get in front of my car, I'm hittin' yo' ass."

The look in my eyes had to warn him that I was as serious as a heart attack and a deadly stroke at the same time. He backed off as I hit the gas and hightailed it out of there. Heading back to my mother's, I wished I'd never ran into him. Atlanta wasn't that big, and something told me that I'd unexpectedly see him, or even Chloe.

If I saw that bitch Chloe, I didn't know what I'd do to her. Yeah, five years had passed, but it was still something in me that wanted her to feel what I had felt that night. I didn't want to just physically hurt her. I wanted to rip her whole world apart and watch her deal with it. That was what she and Eddie had done to me. Their selfish act had changed my life forever.

Yeah, I'd told Eddie that getting away from him was the best decision I'd made in my life and it was. The thing was, going to Florida was something totally different. If only I'd had other options, because damn, Florida was where the plot really began to thicken.

* * *

Miami
2012

After two months in Miami I'd already been exposed to some wild shit. My life in Atlanta was pretty damn tamed, but my cousin Rosita and her mom lived a totally different lifestyle. Sita like me, was an only child. Her mother was my mom's younger sister and like her, she depended on men financially. However, my aunt wasn't hooking on the streets; she was a professional gold digger.

At the age of thirty-six she'd never worked a real job in her life. She'd obviously passed that way of life down to her daughter, who in turn called herself teaching me the ropes. Although Eddie had money, he was broke compared to the niggas that Sita knew. I wasn't accustomed to using a man. I mean, Eddie was there for me financially, but I really loved him for him.

Sita was very pretty and the split image of her mother. Not only did they look alike, but their personalities were similar too. Although I looked like my mother, I was nothing like her. Me and Sita had the same caramel complexion, but her almond shaped eyes were darker than mine and more sinister. My eyes were a lighter brown and I had deep dimples. My nose was a little sharp and hers was more bulbous. Her once long hair was cut in a short pixie style and dyed a bright red. The sexy, curly style fit her feisty, edgy personality to a tee.

It was a warm Saturday evening and me and Sita were perched on the bleachers at a ball park, watching a baseball game played by a local league. There were fine niggas everywhere. Neither of us were watching the game. According to Sita, we were hunting for a different type of "baller".

"See that brown-skinned nigga over there in the red hat?" As she asked, she fanned herself with a napkin.

It was hot as hell. Shit, I thought Atlanta got hot. Following her eyes, I spotted a fine brown-skinned dude with a nice smile and straight, white teeth.

"Uh huh," I nodded. "What about him?"

"Don't stare bitch." Rolling her eyes, she continued. "I used to fuck wit' him back in the day, but he's a dud. He ain't gettin' no real money, so stay away from his thirsty ass. I see he keeps lookin' over here and shit. His brother Leon though, now he gets to that paper." Smiling, she exposed her four iced out bottom teeth.

"That's all you and your mama care about." Shaking my head, I was tired of all the talk about money. Especially when I didn't have any. I'd already spent most of the money I came there with.

"What the fuck else is there to care about? Huh? A nigga?" Sita laughed mockingly. "You should already know that's some bullshit. You see where that got yo' ol' naive ass. Right here for me to school you. All them niggas care about is gettin' their dicks wet. Why not make them pay to play in the waters? Might as well get them sorry mufuckas 'fore they get us. Shit. You won't catch me out here lookin' like no nigga's fool while he fucks this and that bitch. Hell nah."

Regardless of what he'd done, I missed the fuck out of Eddie. I missed Alicia and Margie too. Shit, to be honest, I kind of missed Chloe. She was the one I'd always call to talk shit about Eddie to, because Alicia was neutral. Now I knew that although she'd talked shit with me, she wanted what was mine the entire time. The fact that Eddie allowed her to break us apart was what really hurt me the most. Why the fuck couldn't he have defied that shit? A man I'd loved and cherished for so long fucked up a good thing with me just to get some new pussy. It was my so-called friend's pussy at that. Talk about adding insult to injury. He'd claimed that she came on to him in the many texts he'd sent, but that was no excuse. I'd finally decided to change my number and move on.

Sita kept right on talking. "Why the fuck you think yo' mama do what she do? She need the money bitch. Every woman got a pussy and a man'll pay for it. Hoeing is the oldest profession in the world. Even hoes were in the damn Bible. Shit, it don't take much to make a nigga nut, so... Easy money is the easiest to spend."

Although I couldn't help but agree, I wasn't ready to involve myself with another man in any way. Money wasn't even enough to push me, and I damn sure needed some money. I'd been looking for a job, but according to my aunt and cousin, we were Queens who should be taken care of.

Honestly, as heart-broken as I was, I was horny as fuck. It had been two months since I left Atlanta. A bitch was used to getting some dick on a regular. Eddie still had my head twisted with his head board banging sex and he ate pussy like it was a dessert. Not only that, but damn, I'd loved that man with everything in me. Sita brought men over on a regular and Aunt B had her share of visitors too. I could hear them going at it in their bedrooms as I lie on the sofa with a pillow over my head. Damn, it was time for me to at least meet some nigga to get my mind off Eddie.

"Where's dude brother at? Maybe I should get wit' him then," I said wiping the sweat from my face.

"That nigga ain't gon' be at no baseball game. He got too much swag to sweat out this bitch. Plus, he too busy gettin' to the money."

Rolling my eyes, I asked, "So, why are we here if the "ballers" you talkin' 'bout ain't here?" Shit, I was confused.

"I didn't say that bitch. Just chill out. Believe me, I got some shit up my sleeve. There's some real money out here and we 'bout to cash in."

She had a big shit eating grin on her face. It was like I could see the dollar signs in her eyes as she moved closer to whisper in my ear.

"See that fine ass dude over there on the bottom bleacher with the black True Religion shirt on."

Once I spotted him, I nodded.

"Now, that nigga's bankin'. His name's Rob and that sexy ass chocolate nigga wit' him is Cam. They close as fuck 'cause they grew up together and shit. Yo, them niggas two of the craziest, wildest, most outlandish niggas 'round this mufucka. They both paid as fuck, but Rob runs shit. I heard they be robbin' banks and all. I'm tryna fuck wit' them cats for sho'. Lil' cuz, we gon' get 'em..."

Staring at the two men, I couldn't help but notice how fine they were, but my cousin was nuts. There was no way in hell I was fucking with a nigga who robbed banks. Cam was sexy as shit though, damn. He was black as night with beautiful, silky smooth skin. Mmm, he looked like an African King as he stood there. He had a bunch of iced out chains on and a diamond embezzled watch adorned his wrist. His flawless face was framed by neatly trimmed facial hair and a perfect beard. His close haircut was shaped up and flowed in deep waves. Shit, I was damn near dizzy just by looking at his ass. With full lips, a keen nose, thick brows and "chinky" deep brown eyes, I couldn't look away.

"Cam is sexy as fuck cuz, but I don't know. They be robbin' banks. That's some crazy shit. You sure you wanna deal wit' that?"

"Bitch bye. Eddie's a fuckin' drug dealer and you lived wit' him. What's the damn difference? Long as you ain't doin' that shit, you ain't got shit to worry 'bout. A nigga who breaks the law is a nigga who breaks the fuckin' law." Shrugging her shoulders, she rolled her eyes at me in frustration.

She did have a point, but I was still skeptical about that shit. That nigga was just too damn fine to pass up though, so I relented against my will. It was time to tread into unknown territory. "Well, if we gon' do this, I want Cam."

"So, I wanted Rob any damn way. He's the head nigga in charge. I like a nigga who's powerful enough to run a whole empire. Shit, I need a leader, like me."

Shaking my head, I couldn't help but think about how full of herself Sita was. She'd gotten that from her mother though. That was without a doubt.

After the game was over, Rosita explained that she'd conveniently parked right beside Rob's whip. We waited in her car for them to return to the black SUV. That nigga Rob had to be getting it by any means necessary because the Mercedes SUV was decked out with rims, tint, and a custom platinum grill.

When I spotted them coming our way, Sita sounded excited as she spoke. "Remember cuz, it don't matter how fine that nigga is, how much game he got, or how much money he'll spend, don't get your feelings involved. Just keep tellin' yourself that he's a nigga and he ain't shit like the rest of 'em. All he's worth is the money in his stash. You got it?"

With a nod, I pretended to be on the same page as she was. However, I had no experience with any nigga other than Eddie. Shit, I didn't know how to use a man. Just trying to be sexy was a task for me. I was just used to being myself.

"A'ight, let's get out and pop the hood up. We gon' pretend like there's something wrong with the car. Now put that short ass skirt to work. Watch me."

We exited the car and she opened the hood. Looking inside, we acted like we were trying to figure out what was wrong.

"Now bend over like this. Use what yo' mama gave you girl. They men and all they see is ass. For that reason and that reason only, they gon' offer to help us."

Sure enough, I heard a deep voice behind us. "Sup ladies? Something wrong wit' the whip?"

I let Sita speak.

"Shit, I'on know." Turning around, she looked up at Rob. "It won't start. Maybe it's just hot."

When I turned around, I noticed that Cam was staring at me. The beaded sweat on his forehead tricked down his face and he wiped it away with a white face towel. The entire time, he didn't take his eyes off me.

"It's definitely hot as hell out here and shit. If it wasn't for some plays I needed to make, I wouldn't be out here." Rob grinned slyly exposing a full grill of platinum and diamonds. "I'm glad I came though, 'cause you sexy as shit. What's yo' name, beautiful?"

"I'm Sita and this is my cousin Xa. She just moved down here from the A. What's your name?" Playing dumb, she acted like she didn't already know who he was.

"I'm Rob and that's my boy Cam."

"Nice meetin' y'all," Rosita drawled in a syrupy sweet, southern accent.

Cam finally spoke up. "Xa... mmm... you mind if we talk in private?" Licking his lips, he rubbed his hands together anxiously. "Rob know all about cars, so he can handle that."

I walked over to him and he led me a few feet away.

"Don't get me wrong ma, you gorgeous as hell, but you gotta be careful out here. You look young as shit. How old are you?"

With a grin, I shook my head. "I'm eighteen, so I'm legal. How old are you?"

He smiled back at me and I was relieved to see that he didn't have a grill like Rob. White teeth were more appealing to me. I guess it didn't matter, because I couldn't fall for him. It was all just a game.

"I'm twenty-one."

The short conversation between us flowed as we exchanged numbers. Sita's words echoed in my head as I stared into Cam's bedroom eyes. He was a man and he couldn't be trusted. All I was to him was a shot of ass and a pretty face.

Rob interrupted us. "Yo', everything's straight. Yo' girl's ready to go."

"A'ight sexy, I'm expectin' a call from you." Cam licked his lips and smiled at me.

Blushing visibly, I flirted the best I could. Shit, I didn't know how. "You'll hear from me. Uh, I haven't seen much of Miami yet, so maybe you can take me out soon."

"Hell yeah," he agreed. "That'll be what's up."

"Well, see you later Rob," Sita said with her eyes all over his frame.

Walking away from Cam with a sexy sway of my hips, I hoped I was enticing him. When I looked back, his eyes were glued to my ass. So, that shit was working. Getting in the car with Sita, I let out a sigh.

"A'ight playa." She grinned at me. "We got a date wit' them tomorrow."

Chapter 3

Atlanta

2017

Glancing in the rearview mirror, I noticed that Eddie was right behind me. I'd been reminiscing so hard, I didn't even notice at first. Part of me wanted to drive past my mother's house, so he wouldn't know where she lived, but fuck it. He wasn't going to give up and I figured he knew where she lived already. I'd just have to continue to let him know that I wasn't interested in fixing anything with his ass. Thankfully, I wouldn't be there that long.

Sighing, I pulled into my mother's driveway and Eddie pulled up behind me. Shaking my head, I got out of my car and headed toward the front door without even acknowledging him. That nigga quickly caught up with me.

"Why the fuck are you followin' me?"

Eddie grabbed my arm and turned me around to face him. There was a huge ass smile on his handsome face. "I love your hair like that Xa. You lookin' real damn good."

I'd just had my coarse, dark brown hair cut in layers. It was shoulder length, but had once flowed down my back. A few years ago, I'd chopped it all off in an attempt to let go of the negativity of my past. Part of that was shedding the long hair that reminded me of my mother.

"Save your compliments Eddie. Like I said before, I didn't come here to see you. I can only forgive one sorry mufucka at a time." Reaching in my purse for the key that my mother gave me, I just wished he'd get the damn point and fuck off.

"Xa, please, just hear me out for a minute."

As I shook my head, I retrieved the house key and unlocked the door.

"Wait Xa, please, Xa… baby…"

By that time, my frustration and impatience started to boil to the surface. "Get out of my face Eddie! Fuck you, nigga! My feelings haven't changed! I hate you now just as much as I hated you five years ago! Now leave me the fuck alone!"

Opening the door, I walked in the house and slammed it behind me without looking back. Glancing through the blinds, I saw him get in his burnt orange Cadillac and drive off. It was a relief, but if he didn't know where my mother lived before, he did now. All I could do was hope he'd stay the fuck away.

My mom was at work, so I decided to sit back on the sofa and watch a movie. Her house was small, but neat and clean. That was a big difference from the environment I'd grown up in. Her boyfriend Jamal seemed to be making a huge difference in her life. The plan was for me to meet him the next day.

My cell phone started ringing in my purse and I got up to fish it out. When I saw the familiar number on my screen, I thought about not answering it, but I did. At least she didn't tell her brother that I was coming to Atlanta. Yeah, I'd reached out to Alicia on Facebook about a month before I made my trip back. I made her promise not to tell Eddie, but fate would have it that I saw him before I saw her.

"Hey Alicia."

"Hey Xa. When am I gonna see you?"

"Maybe tonight. I've only been here since yesterday and I was tired from the drive."

She had filled me in on her life the past five years. She had two little girls by Jermaine. Yes, she had babies by that fool and even married his ass.

"I miss you Xa and you know how I feel about how you just disappeared. I understand though. My brother did hurt you."

"Yeah, but that's in the past though."

"I know." She let out a sigh.

"How 'bout we hit up a spot tonight?" I suggested.

"Girl please. I ain't got no babysitter."

"Uh, where the fuck is your husband?"

"He's workin' overtime."

I wanted to say he was probably working overtime on some pussy, but I kept my thoughts to myself.

"Well, how 'bout you bring the girls over here? I want to meet my nieces."

She had two girls named Jamaica and India. They were one and three years old.

"Umm, I'll see. Eddie just called and told me he saw you."

"Yeah, and I don't want to talk about yo' sorry ass brother."

Alicia had also told me that Eddie had a son who was two years old by this bitch named Chelsea. That hoe was also one that I heard he'd cheated on me with back in the day. The fact that he impregnated her proved that rumor was true. She wasn't satisfied until she got knocked up by him. Sometimes, I would notice her staring at me when we took classes together in school. When I asked her what her problem was, she never said shit. In some ways, I wished I'd nipped that shit in the bud back then and dusted off all those bitches. Then again, that nigga Eddie wasn't worth it.

Alicia had said she didn't think the little boy was Eddie's, but it didn't matter to me either way. She claimed the child looked like this dude named Torrence that Chelsea was also fucking with. Although she loved her alleged nephew, she claimed she wasn't going to get too attached just in case.

"My baby girl's cryin' boo. I'll call you in a few and let you know what I'm gon' do."

"A'ight and please don't tell your brother we talked."

"Will do."

After ending the call, I sat back wondering what was going to unfold over the next few days. A few hours later Alicia came over.

"Jermaine agreed to keep the girls while I stop by for a lil' while," she explained with a bottle of Grey Goose.

That boggled my mind. They were his kids too. Why did he see that as keeping them? Once again, I tried not to be petty. After we made some drinks, we chilled on the front porch and talked.

"So, you been in Florida for five years, but you ain't really filled me in. What's been goin' on wit' you?"

"You bein' nosey now Licia."

Okay, I was being cautious of what I shared, even with her. Life had never been too pretty for me and the past five years had been a true test of the survival of the fittest. I had to learn to hustle and not have a conscience. After what I'd been through, it was best not to have any feelings at all.

Looking like she was taken aback, Alicia said, "Damn, I ain't bein' nosey."

Her hurt facial expression made me feel bad.

"I'm just concerned about you. I missed you and you are my best friend. Shit, I just wondered what happened to you."

"I'm sorry Alicia. Look, what's been goin' on in my life the past few years is just a long, drawn out story. What's important is I'm here now and we are still best friends. We'll talk about all that later. Okay?" Hoping that she'd drop it, I forced a smile on my face.

Shrugging her shoulders, she agreed.

"Whatever girl. You lookin' good. You done put on a few pounds. Hmm, some extra weight looks good on you. Yo' ass was too damn scrawny."

We laughed and then she brought up Eddie.

"He wouldn't stop talkin' 'bout you. He kept talkin' 'bout how thick you got and how he regrets fuckin' up what y'all had. He still loves you Xa."

"That's just too damn bad. I don't love Eddie anymore. He hurt me beyond words, so it's no way I can tell you how he made me feel. As far as I'm concerned, he and Chloe can still kiss my ass. I know he's your brother, but he ripped my heart out of my chest and stumped all over that shit. Fuck him. I'm not proud of the person I have become because of it."

Alicia didn't press the issue. Although she wanted me to go into detail, she didn't pry. She knew we'd talk about it all when I was ready. At about twelve Alicia left, because she'd already explained that she couldn't stay too late. Jermaine had called several times to tell her that their baby girl was awake and wouldn't go back to sleep. He claimed that Alicia was the one who had spoiled her rotten. The way I saw it, that nigga just wanted her to come home.

"I gotta go girl. That girl is spoiled as hell. Her daddy did that shit, not me."

Mmm, that was so he could use her as an excuse to control Alicia's whereabouts.

"Well, call me when you get home." I walked her to the door and watched as she got in her car and drove off.

Not too long after, she called to let me know that she'd made it home. It was a Friday night and I was bored as hell. My mother had to work a double shift and wouldn't be home until the sun came up. The Publix she worked at was open twenty four hours.

The glare of headlights pulling into the driveway brightened the room and bounced off the wall. Who the hell could that possibly be? Was my mother home early? I peeked out of the window and saw that it was Eddie's car. As I watched, he stepped out of his car and boldly proceeded to the front door. It was as if I didn't tell him that I didn't want to deal with his ass earlier. The doorbell rang, and I asked who it was as if I didn't know.

"It's me, Eddie."

"Go away, Eddie."

"Xa, we need to talk. Open the door."

"Oh my God. It is five years too late for that. Please, just do me a favor and let it go. Whatever we had is over, so just leave the past in the past."

There was the faint sound of a heavy sigh. Even the sound of his shoes as he paced back and forth could be heard.

"Xa, I didn't think I'd ever see you again. I made the biggest mistake of my life when I fucked

Chloe. I regret that shit and I can't let it be. I love you and I never once stopped. Real shit. I never will."

I promised myself that I'd never let a man hurt me again. There was no way that I'd let Eddie repeat history. Even if he was sincere, I wasn't willing to take that risk to find out. I'd become the player, not the one to get played.

"You didn't think about all that when yo' dick was up in that bitch, so I don't want to hear it. To be honest, that shit really don't matter now. It was five years ago and I'm over it. You should get over it too. Shit, I got my share of niggas to keep me occupied. I don't even have time to entertain you and your regrets."

"Oh really?"

"Nigga, you act like it's hard to believe."

"I'on know. I mean, after the shit you went through as a lil' girl, I ain't think you'd want to fuck wit' a bunch of niggas and shit."

"Well, being that you know what I went through as a lil' girl, I ain't think you would hurt me like you did. Guess neither of us really knew the other."

Though I was defiant, he still stirred something deep inside of me. However, I hid it well.

"I know I can't take it back, but damn Xa, I made a mistake..."

"Look, I've been through enough bullshit to write a fuckin' bestseller and I don't give a fuck about you or any other nigga. That's the difference between the girl you knew and the woman I am now. That girl cared about you. The night she caught you fuckin' her best friend was the night she went away and was replaced by me. I'm the one who don't give a fuck about you. So, fuck the past and your so-called mistake, Eddie. It don't mean shit to me."

"Damn, I was young and stupid. C'mon Xa. I had a weak moment, but that don' take away from the love I felt for you. I still feel that same love baby. You wasn't tryna fuck me like I needed and I had my needs. I guess that sounds like a lame ass excuse and it don't matter what I say, but..."

"It don't matter! Your apologies don't mean shit to me! You're gettin' on my fuckin' nerves Eddie. Forget about me! Go see some bitch who really gives a fuck about you!"

"You the only woman I give a fuck about Xa, I swear."

Opening the door, I figured that if he saw that I was serious, he'd get the fuck on. "If you don't get off this damn porch!"

Without warning, he grabbed me and kissed me. Trying to pull away, I felt his warm tongue enter my mouth. Although I wanted to defy the passion that was still lingering between us, I couldn't. Against my better judgment, I found myself enjoying it. Eddie softly sucked on my bottom lip before pulling away.

Damnit, why did I let him finish that kiss? He'd think I wanted him to do that shit!

"Why the fuck did you do that?" Wiping my mouth, I gave him a cold look.

"Had to. I missed kissin' those sweet, sexy lips."

"Your ass is so fuckin' disrespectful. I didn't want you to kiss me, so don't get that shit twisted. If you touch me again, I'm gon' cut you."

The comforting melody of his laughter reminded me of the good times we'd shared.

"You know you liked that shit. You almost shoved your tongue down my throat. Don't front. You still love me, don't you?"

It was more of a statement than a question. Looking up at him, I had a smirk on my face.

"I figured that if I kissed you back, you'd let me go."

"You won't admit it. That's not good."

Rolling my eyes, I told him, "I'm goin' in the house now Eddie. Have a nice life and don't show up over here again!"

"A'ight, I'll just let you simmer on that kiss. Think about how good I used to eat that..."

Closing the door on his ass, I locked it and returned to the sofa. As much as that kiss had made me weak, there was no way I'd ever go there with him again. All the good memories were overshadowed by that one bad one. There was no way I could risk those old feelings returning. Trust was out of the question when it came to Eddie and besides, I wasn't planning to stay in Atlanta anyway.

Furthermore, I'd convinced myself that love wasn't for me anyway. Maybe it never was. I used men for my benefit and that was it. Like Sita had told me, I didn't get my feelings involved anymore. I'd learned my lesson the hard way. All I wanted to do was work on rebuilding a relationship with my mother. The rest of that shit was for the birds.

* * *

The next day my mom had the day off and it was time for me to meet her boo. Jamal seemed like a real nice guy, despite what I thought about the opposite sex. My stomach was growling, and he was starting up the grill. It was after six o' clock and I was hungry as shit. Ma reassured me that he was an excellent cook.

"That man is everything." She beamed as she poured us both a glass of lemonade.

Of course, I wanted something stronger, but she didn't drink anymore. She'd made homemade lemonade, which was one more thing I'd been deprived of as a child.

"You two seem really happy ma. I'm glad you met him. Shit, he sure beats the mess you used to bring home."

Tears stung my eyes. During the times we'd conversed since I moved to Florida, we never discussed the past. That was a conversation that couldn't be avoided. I needed closure in order to heal, but I wasn't ready to have that talk.

"Well Xa, we all do things that we regret in life. I have to deal with the past every day. Jamal is the only person who'll let me forget it. All he cares about is the future."

She looked at me and our eye contact lingered. I watched as she squirmed uncomfortably in her seat. "I can't blame it all on the alcohol. I loved money. I loved to look good and have nice things. More than alcohol, money was my addiction. I just needed to drink to do what I had to do to get it and it got out of control. I was young, and I didn't want to be a single mother. I didn't realize how precious you were until I woke up one morning sober as hell. I hadn't been sober in a while. My mind was finally clear and all I could think about was you, baby girl. That's when I knew that I had to make sure I stayed clean. I met Jamal about a week later and he helped me get in a good treatment program. It was clear that just not drinking wasn't going to solve my problems. I needed to get healthy mentally too. I can't change the fact that I was a bad mother to you, but I can let you know how sorry I am. If I could take all of it away from you baby girl, I would. Instead of protecting you, I put you in harm's way." Wiping the tears from her eyes, she continued. "I hated myself for that for a long time. I'm just glad you don't seem to hate me as much. I'm sure at some point you did. I'm blessed to have you here wit' me after all I did." Leaning over, she planted a kiss on my forehead.

"I don't hate you at all, ma" I told her.

She smiled and stood up. "I invited Alicia and the girls over. They are so precious. I even watch them for her sometimes when I'm off work. It gives me a chance to be responsible. Maybe one day you'll give me some grandbabies."

"Not anytime soon."

We both laughed.

"Well, take your time baby girl."

"Mmm, mama, you don't even curse like you used to. You had a foul mouth back in the day."

"Well, me and Jamal go to Mt. Zion when we can. It's so many other words to use to express yourself. Ain't no need to curse."

That impressed me. Jamal grinned at us as he flipped the burgers over. I couldn't help but notice the affection between them. Almost an hour had passed by before people started to arrive. I didn't know that my mom had invited anybody other than Alicia and her babies. I'd almost forgotten that black people invited themselves to cookouts. All I could do was hope Eddie didn't show up.

Finally, Alicia showed up with Jermaine and their adorable little girls.

"This is Auntie Xa. Say hi," Alicia told them as she grinned proudly.

"Hi Auntie Xa," they said in unison showing dimples.

The one year old didn't say it as clearly of course.

"Hi little cuties." I hugged them both.

"How you doin' Xa?" Jermaine asked. "It's been a minute." He looked the same, but was a bit heavier. Alicia must've been feeding him good.

"I'm fine Jermaine. How are you?"

"Wonderful bein' that yo' girl done made me the happiest man in the world."

"Take them babies over there and get them some food Jermaine," ma said shoving them off.

Giving Alicia a glance, she nodded and walked away.

"Uh, Xa, look... I know that what Chloe did hurt you..."

"Alicia, where the hell are you going with this?" I stared at her blankly as I cut her off.

"Chloe's really sorry about what happened. She told me earlier today that you ain't never give her a chance to apologize."

"Umm, so why you tellin' me this shit?"

"Shhh." Alicia put her index finger to her lips and looked around. "Umm, Chloe's in the car."

"What?" I shrieked. "What the fuck you mean that bitch's in the car? No, you didn't invite that skank ass hoe over here."

"Lower your voice Xa, damn. Don't make a scene. I didn't invite her. Your mom did."

Shaking my head, I said, "If I see that bitch I'm gon' hurt her. Time and space ain't changed shit. I don't care about her or Eddie. As far as I'm concerned, they don't fuckin' exist."

With that said, I walked away from Alicia. Jermaine ended up taking Chloe home.

"You trust that slut alone wit' your man?" I asked Alicia.

"Shit, they both know better. I'll chop both them mufuckas up and spread the pieces all over the United States."

"Damn bitch. You crazier than me."

"Chloe done changed Xa. She been through a lot. You two are a lot alike you know. You got more in common than you think."

"Yeah, like Eddie's dick," I threw in sarcastically.

"Stop."

"I ain't nothing like that bitch. You stop." Squeezing ketchup on a hotdog, I realized that I didn't even want it.

"I think you should at least give her a chance to talk to you."

"What's that shit gonna solve Alicia? I still wanna hurt that bitch. If I see her, I might just do it."

"See, that's why you need to face her. To finally get over that anger. It's been too long for you to still be holding on to that shit. Resolve it."

"Well, it wouldn't be that easy for you to say if it was Jermaine who fucked her and not Eddie. She was my best friend other than you. She ain't shit and I choose not to deal wit' her. Now drop it. Case closed Alicia."

She shrugged her shoulders and bit into her burger. "Shit, okay."

Chapter 4

Florida

2013

For a few months I'd been playing Cam, but I realized that I wasn't playing at all. My dumb, sensitive ass was starting to catch feelings. I'd learned to try and suppress those emotions to get what I wanted with no strings attached. There was no way I could let myself get caught up. However, using men wasn't my only scheme.

Aunt B had a friend who worked for a telemarketing company. Her name was Gloria and she was also driven by money and greed. She would steal the credit card numbers of her clients and tape them on the back of expired, or dummy credit cards.

The scheme went like this; we had to go to a cashier who was in on that shit. They'd swipe the card first and then pretend like something was wrong. They'd type in the numbers that were taped on the back of the card and voila! That was how we purchased a lot of the expensive shit we had. We'd only use each card number once and spend thousands. Most of the time we used the cards for online purchases, because that was more discreet.

Since Gloria and Aunt B were cool, she didn't have to pay her much for the numbers.

Gloria got paid, we got shopping sprees and in case Aunt B's niggas didn't want to pay up, the bills were paid.

Aunt B and Sita had plenty of tricks up their sleeves. They'd often buy expensive outfits, wear them once with the tags tucked in and then return them. After they got off on wearing that shit, they'd get a refund, or exchange. Yeah, they were crafty. Although they didn't work for it, they had the finer things in life. When I was younger, I always wondered how. Why couldn't my mother have had it together like Aunt B?

My cell phone rang.

"Hey baby," I answered chewing on some strawberry banana Bubblicious bubble gum.

"Hey brown sugar," Cam said. His voice made me melt instantly.

After I blew a bubble, I smiled. "What's goin' on bae?"

"Shit, what's goin' on wit' you?"

"Nothing. Sittin' here waitin' for the damn bus. It's late as usual." I made sure to sound as annoyed as I felt.

In a short amount of time, I'd managed to wrap Cam around my little finger. Somehow, I had learned how to be seductive, manipulative and conning. Although I was quite fond of Cam, I was determined to not get caught up. There was no way, especially not after Eddie.

"I'll come get you babe. Where you at?"

After I told him where I was, we hung up.

My phone blared again about fifteen minutes later.

"Yeah."

"Wha' gwaan empress?" A sexy Jamaican accent greeted my ears.

"Is this my original don dotta?"

I'd met Rahz a month earlier. He was Jamaican and damn if he wasn't fine and paid out the ass. With skin the color of Brazilian coffee beans, gray eyes and thick lips, he made me feel some type of way. You should know by now that I had a thing for dark skinned men.

"Yuh know star. How's my sugar dumplings?"

"I'm good. How 'bout you?"

"Shit, just sittin' here tinkin' 'bout yuh."

Mmm, I loved his accent and his long dreadlocks. The way his edges curled up just did something to me.

"Aww, that's sweet Rahz. You makin' me blush."

"You goin' wit' me to New York next month?" He'd been asking for the past few days.

"I'on know. I don't think I can take off from work," I whined.

The truth was, I didn't have a job yet. I just told niggas that shit so they'd want to help me. A man wanted to help a woman that he thought really didn't need it. Well, that was what Aunt B had told me.

"Try to take di time off anyway. I'll give yuh di money yuh would've made. Shit, if yuh let a nigga take care of yuh, yuh won't have to work."

"I like takin' care of myself, but thank you." The lie slipped off my tongue so easily.

Rahz was already under my spell. After a few more minutes of talking, I spotted Cam's white Lexus LX with the butterscotch interior. That shit was fire as hell.

"Look, I'm gonna call you later baby. I have to get back to work."

"Okay beautiful."

Ending the call quickly, I stood up. Cam rolled down his window and licked his luscious lips. "Get in baby girl."

Once I was seated in the passenger seat, I kissed his soft lips.

"Damn, that outfit looks good on you."

"Thanks for gettin' it for me baby."

"Anything for yo' bad ass. Mmm... I gotta be honest 'bout some shit. You too damn fine to be at a bus stop. I gotta get you a whip."

"No, I can't let you do that. We only been dealin' for..."

Putting a finger to my lips he said, "Time don't matter ma. I can't have my lady ridin' no bus and shit."

"Okay..." With an innocent look on my face, I turned and peered out of the window. That was when a sly grin spread across my face. "Because it be some thirsty ass niggas on the bus."

"You comin' home wit' me?"

"I 'on know..."

"What you mean you don't know. I'm tryna get some of that good ass pussy. All I been thinkin' 'bout is you ridin' me..."

"All you think about is fuckin'." Shaking my head, I glanced over at him.

Cam reached in his pocket and pulled out a wad of bills. "Here," he said placing them in my hand. "Now, what you gotta say?"

"Nothing."

Smiling victoriously, he drove off.

All I had to do was fuck him good and play that sweet, innocent role with just enough freak. It wasn't hard to do, especially when the dick was good. The thing was, Cam had some real damn drama in his life and her name was Ebony. She was his baby's mama and a pain in my ass. We'd only crossed paths once and although neither of us said anything, the tension was mad thick.

Their daughter Camille was two years old. She was adorable, but spoiled and bad as hell. Cam had her the next weekend. It was like he couldn't go a day without getting some of this pussy, so once Camille was sleep, I dropped by.

"Damn, you know you lookin' right, like always." He greeted me at the door with a sly grin on his face.

Mmm, as much as I didn't want to be feeling him, Cam made me go against all that.

"And you lookin' and smellin' right, like always," I whispered seductively in his ear. As I did, I nibbled softly on his earlobe.

"I'm 'bout to have yo' fine ass feelin' right, like always. C'mon." Grabbing my hand, he led me up the stairs of his plush two-story home with a finished basement.

Camille was sleep, so it was cool to do what we had to do. When she was there, I'd only come through when she was in bed. That wasn't Cam's decision though. In his eyes, I was his woman, so he wanted me to have a relationship with his daughter. Me on the other hand, I wasn't trying to get attached to his child, because I wasn't in it for the long haul. All I wanted was what he was willing to provide and in case that shit was temporary, I didn't want to bond with Camille. Besides, she was spoiled rotten, so that wasn't difficult.

Once we were in his bedroom, Cam didn't waste his time talking. He slowly removed my clothes and as he did, his eyes were glued to my body.

"Damn, you blessed ma." His voice was breathless as he kissed my neck and then collarbone.

His tongue moved down to my nipples and then to my bellybutton. After teasing me relentlessly, he told me to lie down. When I was on my back, he continued to bestow sweet kisses down my anatomy. After sucking on my toes, his tongue slid up my leg and inner thigh. Then, he started feasting on my pussy.

"Ohhh... Cam... shit..." My eyes rolled back in pleasure as he devoured my hard clit with sucks and slurps.

Next thing I knew, two of his long, thick fingers were deep inside of me.

As my leg trembled and the warm tingles started, I knew it was over for me. My juices flowed onto his tongue as I held on to the back of his head and locked him in place.

"Shit..." My legs stiffened, and I pushed his head away because that shit was too damn intense.

He didn't let up. Instead, he locked my ass cheeks in place and kept right on eating me out.

"I can't take it anymore... ohhh... uhhh... Cam..." My hand was pushing against his forehead, but that nigga wouldn't budge.

Four orgasms later, and I was ready to jump on that nigga's dick. Letting my aggressive side out, I pushed him back on the bed and put the condom on for him. One thing I wasn't playing was that raw shit. I didn't know who else that nigga was fucking.

"When you gon' let me hit that thang without a damn rubber?" He asked as I straddled him and grabbed his dick.

Placing it at the tip of my entrance, I slid down slowly, contracting my muscles as I did. That nigga grabbed my waist and his eyes rolled back.

As I grinded on top of him, moving my body like a sexy serpent, he gripped my waist. Then I leaned over and kissed him sweetly.

"You can hit it without a rubber when you put a ring on it."

That nigga cuffed my thighs with his strong hands and squeezed. "Keep ridin' my dick like that and I might just do that shit. Mmm… dayum…"

* * *

The next morning, I woke up to the sound of loud banging. Somebody was obviously knocking on the door and it wasn't even eight o' clock yet.

"What the fuck?" Cam asked groggily.

When the banging didn't stop, he lifted his warm body from the bed and threw on some sweat pants. Turning over on my stomach, I grabbed the pillow and closed my eyes. Before I could drift back off, I heard a woman's voice.

"I know she's here Cam! Why do you keep havin' that bitch around my daughter when I told you constantly not to? Huh? Fuck this shit man! Go wake my baby up!"

That hoe was loud enough for me to hear her upstairs, so I was sure her baby was already awake. Loud, petty ass bitch. Well, I could be even louder and pettier. In less than sixty seconds I was dressed and headed down the stairs. Then I was up in her face before Cam knew what was coming.

"Who the fuck you callin' a bitch, bitch? You don't fuckin' know me. I'll fuck yo' ass up in here.

I'on give a fuck how many damn babies you got wit' him."

Cam suddenly stood between us and it was in good timing. I was just about to haul off and chin check that bitch. She had too much damn mouth and I was the one to shut that hoe up.

"C'mon Xa and chill the fuck out Eb. You can go in the room and get Camille. After that, I want yo' disrespectful ass to leave."

"I'm disrespectful, but you the one who be trippin' 'bout me havin' a nigga around Camille? Fuck you Cam. You ain't shit. If you keep on fuckin' wit' her, you ain't gon' see yo' daughter no more. She told me how she treats her."

"How I treat her? Stop makin' up shit. I'm hardly even around your daughter." It was taking everything in me not to slap that bitch.

"And I told you that," Cam cosigned.

"What the fuck ever nigga. We both know that you'll be right back in my face tryna fuck. I'on know why you frontin' on that fake shit 'round her."

"Is this 'bout her bein' around Camille or the fact that she's gettin' the dick? 'Cause you already know ain't nobody tryna get no more of that tired ass pussy."

That made me laugh out loud.

"Tired ass pussy, but you nutted in me though? Nigga, please stop. You just makin' yourself look stupid."

"Nah, you look stupid. The pussy's tired 'cause I don't want it no more. It ain't worth hearin' yo' fuckin' mouth, or dealin' wit' yo' annoyin' ass. The only thing we ever need to talk about is our daughter. I ain't fucked yo' ass in over a year. You the one frontin'."

"Nigga, stop playin'." She rolled her eyes and sucked her teeth. "You know you be beggin' to fuck."

"Oh, shit, man. You really delusional as fuck. The last time we fucked, you was beggin' for the D. Look, we ain't got shit between us, but our baby girl. What I do ain't none of yo' business. Now, if you want to take Camille home, do what you gotta do. Just get the fuck outta here. The only pussy I'm beggin' for is right here wit' me."

Ebony went off after that and started punching him in the chest. Without even thinking about it, I grabbed that bitch by her shirt and pulled her away from him. "Get the fuck off him, bitch!"

"Bitch, you gon' make me beat yo' fuckin' ass!" She yelled at me.

"C'mon then bitch. I been waitin' for a reason to..." I was squared up.

"Babe, fuck all that. Okay? My baby's in there." Holding me back, Cam tried to reason with me.

"Tell that ignorant ass bitch that. She's the one all in her feelings 'cause you ain't fuckin' her no more."

"Girl, you just temporary just like all the rest of them hoes. We'll be right back together after he drops yo' ass."

"Oh, so you his rebound pussy, huh? You the one he fucks when nobody else is around. Hah, bitch. He got that platinum, million-dollar pussy now. He won't be needin' your charity pussy anymore. Sorry."

She grunted and lunged toward me, but once again Cam kept us from fighting. That shit pissed me off, because I wanted to take out all my frustration on her face. When she realized that our efforts to throw hands were in vain, she walked off to get her daughter.

"I ain't got time for this bullshit," she threw over her shoulder.

Camille was still asleep when she returned to the room.

"Let me give my baby a kiss," Cam told her.

Ebony turned their daughter away from him. "Nigga, you done lost yo' mufuckin' mind. You probably just ate that bitch's nasty ass pussy. You ain't puttin' yo' mouth on my baby."

"You right hoe, he damn sure did eat my pussy. He ate it good too. You mad 'cause he ain't eatin' that fish tank you got?"

Ebony gave me the evil eye. "You better be glad I'm holdin' my daughter."

"No bitch, you better be glad you holdin' your daughter. Don't do me, 'cause you can put her down and get these damn hands."

Really, I didn't give a shit about being with Cam. I just didn't like the bitch he'd chose to knock up.

"Stop it now, both of you. Don't do this shit 'round Camille. Damn." Cam shook his head and glared at me, then Ebony.

That hoe rolled her eyes and left without saying another word.

"What the fuck man?" Cam asked me once he locked the door.

"Don't come at me like that hoe didn't come for me wit' that bitch shit."

As he sighed, he ran his hand over his smooth, wavy hair. "You could've been more mature about it."

"Why the fuck do I have to be the mature one when yo' ignorant ass baby mama disrespected me first?"

Cam shook his head and wrapped his arms around my waist. His hands dropped down to my ass.

"Look, fuck that. She wants us to fuss and shit, but I really want some more of that pussy. Now that Camille's gone, you can get as loud as you want."

Yawning, I stretched and shook my head. "Nah babe. I'm goin' back to sleep."

"I know Eb messed up the mood, but I don't want her. I mean that shit."

Waving him off, I headed toward the bedroom. "I don't give a fuck about that bitch."

When I walked in the room, I headed straight for the bed and climbed under the covers. Cam got in the bed and snuggled close to me like some sucker. I wasn't with all that lovey dovey shit. That would only mess up my mission of keeping my heart out of the equation.

"You ain't even gotta move baby. I'll do all the work. Just let me feel you, please."

His soft, warm lips were on my neck.

That shit made me smile. If only his baby mama could hear him begging me for the pussy.

Grinding my ass into him was my invite. He removed my panties and stirred up my wetness with his finger. I wanted him to go ahead and put it in. Fuck all that teasing shit.

"Just go ahead, nigga. I'm sleepy as fuck."

"Why you always act like that when a nigga try and touch you. All you ever want is yo' pussy ate and some dick."

"Nigga, why you complainin'? It ain't like you love me."

He had a hurt look on his face. "Just go back to sleep yo'."

Was that nigga catching feelings? I damn sure hoped he wasn't. For some reason, despite what I'd been through and all that Sita was trying to teach me, I felt bad. Cam came off like a hard ass nigga, but he wore his heart on his sleeve at times.

Only wanting that good dick and money made me start seeing him as just an object, not a person. What I'd been through in the past made it easier for me to live by Sita's philosophy. My goal was to just do what was best for me. Fuck anybody else's feelings. My heart was slowly turning into ice.

"Cam, look, don't be like that. I just... I've been through some shit that makes me not trust men. I told you that. Plus, you ain't never expressed any kind of feelings for me."

"I might not've said the words, I love you, but I express my feelings for you. Why do you think I go out of my way for yo' ass? I might not be the most verbal nigga, but I show how I feel. I ain't askin' you to trust me Xa. Let me earn it. Just let me get closer to you and I'll prove that you can trust me. Shit, you too damn fine to pass up. For real ma."

So, I made sure he slid on a condom and it was on. For the second time, he banged my back out just right. Once we were done, I was spent, so in no time I was out like a light. I woke up at about eleven and there was a text from Cam.

I'll be right back beautiful. Make yourself comfy. It's plenty of food in the fridge.

Wondering what was up with him, I did help myself to a fresh croissant with sliced turkey and cheese. There was a pot of coffee that he'd brewed before he left that was still piping hot. Shit, I needed that to wake my ass up. That nigga had worn me out. After I ate, I went upstairs to use the master bathroom.

Cam texted me again, and as I sat on the toilet, I checked the message.

Don't leave. Take a shower and put on one of my big tee shirts. I'm out buyin you some underwear and a few outfits. Don't worry. I know your sizes. We going out of town later.

My heart skipped a beat as a giddy smile crept on my face. Although I wouldn't allow myself to love Cam, I did love the fact that he was full of surprises. He was definitely not like Eddie. I had to go out of my way to make sure I kept my heart out of our little affair. I'd never love another man again and I'd make sure of it.

Chapter 5

Atlanta

2017

Man, a bitch was so confused. As much as I had bad memories of home, the nostalgic feeling made me not want to go back to Florida. Maybe I was searching for something and I didn't know where to find it. Instead of dwelling on it, I decided to take myself out to eat. My mother was at work and as much as I loved Alicia, I wasn't in the mood to talk about her brother or Chloe.

I found myself at Ihop. A t-bone, eggs and pancakes would be on the money. My waitress ended up being an old classmate named Shannon. We were never close, but she was pretty cool. Unlike the other kids, she didn't fuck with me, so I didn't have any animosity towards her.

"Girl, I ain't seen you in years." As she recognized me she smiled.

Returning her show of kindness, I smiled too. She looked the same, brown skinned with a short haircut and pretty smile. "I been gone girl. I had to get away."

"I know what you mean. I tried college, but it wasn't for me. I been back now for 'bout three years. Now I'm ready to go. I'm workin' two jobs tryna save up. I got a little boy now and well, I want to make sure he has a good life. I've been thinkin' about movin' up top. I got family in Connecticut."

"You gotta do you."

With a nod, she made small talk as she took my order. I grubbed and before I left, we exchanged numbers to keep in touch. Knowing me, I wasn't going to call her.

When I returned to my mom's, I was full and bored as hell. Plopping on the sofa, I turned on the TV. Although I had nothing in particular to do or nobody to see, it felt good. In Florida, I had way too much to do. Peace and quiet was not a part of my life there, so I was actually enjoying the feeling.

My phone rang and I ignored it. The caller decided to call right back though. I looked at the screen and it was Sita.

"What's up bitch? Why y'en called me since you been gone?" Her rude ass asked.

"Ain't shit up and you ain't my mama, my boss, or my nigga, so why you questionin' me?"

"Shut the fuck up. When you comin' back?"

"I'on know when I'll be back, but you ain't gotta worry 'bout me stayin' here too long. I miss all the drama."

We both laughed.

"You crazy, bitch. Solo been askin' 'bout you too. That nigga's feelin' yo' ass. C'mon, you gotta get over Cam. He wasn't your man anyway. Plus, yo' ass wasn't supposed to catch feelings."

"Do you hear yourself bitch? What? I wasn't supposed to feel shit? What happened was because of me!" Tears burned my eyes, but I wiped them away before they could fall.

Sita finally spoke. "I'm sorry." Clearing her throat, she added, "I can be a lil' cold at times. I was raised that way cuz. Real shit though. It's time to move on. The past is just that, the past. Leave it there. It's been years now."

"I know, but that doesn't change it." Sitting up, I wished I hadn't even answered Sita's call.

"Anywho, back to that nigga Solo. Don't pass him up Xa. You need to step yo' game back up. You been fuckin' wit' Ramon's black ass too long and he ain't even on the same level as Solo. He ain't shit but a pretty boy, petty hustler. I mean, the dick is probably good as hell, but you can still get it and get a nigga wit' a bigger bank roll."

Not able to help it, I laughed. "Tell Aunt B I said hi, but I gotta go."

"Bitch… what you gotta say 'bout what I just said?"

Rolling my eyes, I told her, "Ramon's cool people. It ain't just 'bout his dick and he got more money than you think." At some point, I felt like he cared about me at least a little bit, unlike those scoundrels she was fucking with. No wonder she never caught feelings. Why should she?

"Man, fuck carin' cuz. Have you learned anything from me? It's all about gettin' them dollars and that dick. All pleasure and no pain. You need to stop givin' a damn 'bout these lame ass niggas. I already told you why they be actin' like

they care. It's a front until they get what the fuck
they want and you start caring back. Fuck that.
That's why them niggas spend money on designer
clothes and shit. That's why they get nice whips
and rims. Would niggas really sport jewels, or get
grills in they mouths if that shit didn't impress
bitches? Hell nah. All they want is to fuck.
Everything they do is to fuck. Even fuckin' actin' like
they care. So don't be green about that shit. Just
get the green and keep it fuckin' movin'. It's all a
game and we gon' beat them niggas at it."

"A'ight. I gotta go Sita." For once I was sick
of her politics about men and money.

"Well, fuck you too. Bye."

"Stop bein' sensitive hoe."

She laughed. "You ain't fuckin' that nigga
Eddie again are you? Don't be a fool."

"You must've bumped yo' head if you think
I'll ever fuck him again. You a fool for asking me
that shit."

"Well, if you ain't did it yet, you probably
will. The longer you stay there the harder it's gonna
be for yo' ass to resist."

"Bye Sita." And damn if I wanted to hear
that bullshit.

When I hung up, I tried to do what Sita said
and not dwell on my past. It was time for me to
move on, but my past wasn't like most.

* * *

Florida
2013

The months had flown by and I was starting to see Rahz more. In a short time, he was acting as if he was so in love with me. That nigga was spending money on me like water, but for some reason, he'd never put money in my hand. Unlike Cam, Rahz was more romantic and verbally expressive though. You could say that nigga had a way with words. Then, I saw another side of him.

I'd been in Florida for about a year at that point. I'd only been fucking with Rahz sexually for a few months, although we'd been talking for a while. He required a lot of my time, but I still managed to do my thing with Cam. His baby mama drama was a turn off though, so I was seeing him a little less.

After I put it on Rahz's fine ass, he started to become possessive and jealous.

"I ain't yo' woman," I had to remind him after he stole some nigga in the face for looking in me. "Why you actin' all crazy and shit?"

We were downtown at a fancy restaurant and I had to admit I *was* slaying. Rahz grabbed my wrist after punching the dude and pulled me outside to his black Benz. Onlookers watched in shock and a few had pulled out their cellphones prepared to record a fight.

"It's 'cause yuh showin' all yo' ass in that tight ass shit!" He was so angry that his jaw muscle kept twitching.

"Man, yo' ass is on one right now. I ain't tryna do this shit wit' you."

"Fuck dat. Get yo' ass in di fuckin' car!" His eyes were blazing as he stared me down.

"I ain't goin' nowhere wit' you. When you mad, you drive like you tryna kill us both. Nope, you can gone head, but I'm good. I'll get an Uber."

Rahz's eyes looked like they were on fire. "Did a fuckin' Uber bring yuh here? Get in di damn car! Now! Mi a grown fuckin' mon and mi don't 'ave time to play lil' boy games wit' a lil' gyal."

"Leave me the fuck alone Rahz! I'm so serious right now. I'll get home on my own. You can bet yo' life on that shit."

Cam had bought me a whip, but my dumb ass rode with Rahz. Shit, I should've drove my damn self. Mad niggas wanted me, and so I smiled cockily as I thought about my many prospects. I'd established a thorough reputation in Miami. Long gone was the girl that everybody picked on. Rahz could easily be replaced.

"Yuh gon' make mi slap that fuckin' smile off ya face, bitch!"

That nigga had never talked to me like that before and he wasn't about to start. Usually he was saying some sweet, manipulative ass shit that had me fooled. All I could do was shake my head.

"I don't know what the fuck yo' problem is, but you ain't 'bout to be spazin' out on me. You better be glad that nigga didn't whoop yo' ass. As far as you know, he's already called the cops and they're on the way. You know you don't need that type of heat, or did you think about that? I saw that .45 under yo' seat. You want them to find that?"

A look of panic washed over his face, but his voice was calmer. "Look babe, mi can't just be chillin' out here like mi didn't do shit. Yuh right, dat rassclat muthafucka, or management's probably on di phone wit' di cops right now. Let's go."

With my arms across my chest, I told him defiantly, "Go ahead. I ain't feelin' yo' temper and I ain't goin' nowhere wit' you. So, go ahead and drive the fuck off."

"Yuh really tink mi playin' don't yuh?" His face was screwed up into a scowl.

Shrugging my shoulder, I spat, "I don't give a shit. Just go. Damn. First of all, you punched that man in the face for nothin', and then you gon' go off on me 'bout what the fuck I got on. You ain't my fuckin' daddy. That jealous bullshit is a turn off. Stay the fuck away from me."

With an evil smirk on his face, he just stared at me. "Yuh ain't talkin' to me like dat! All mi ever did was be good to yuh. Mi spoil yo' ass and yuh gon' treat mi like dis? Yuh belong to me. Di contract was signed after mi got di pum pum. Dat's right, yo' ass is stuck wit' me fi life, star."

The sound of sirens was heard off in the distance, so I had to fuck with him.

"Whatever, but yo' ass gon' be stuck in prison if you don't get the fuck outta here. Bye Rahz." I waved at him to taunt him even further.

"A'ight, have it yo' way. Calm down, get yourself together and then we'll talk. How yuh gettin' home?"

Rolling my eyes, I just wished he'd leave. "I'll get there. Don't worry 'bout me."

He nodded and played with the thick black hairs on his chin. "Uh huh, so yuh gon' call another nigga to come get yuh?"

"Fuck, you need some serious help. I can't believe you're acting like this. Damn, I should have never fucked you."

Giving me a look like he wanted to cut off my air supply, he shook his head and then drove off screeching tires. Once he was out of sight, I called Cam. I could hear loud music and people talking in the background when he answered.

"Sup baby?"

Maybe he wasn't as expressive as Rahz, but he was damn sure more tolerable.

"Not shit. What you got goin' on?"

"Chillin' wit' the niggas and shit. I'm 'bout to drop them off in a minute. Why? You wanna see a nigga?"

"If you ain't too busy."

"Never too busy for you."

"Well, I'm over here on Jupiter Ave. I'm hungry and wanted to have dinner with you."

Me and Rahz didn't have a chance to eat before he started throwing blows. There were plenty of restaurants on that street.

Cam started coughing. "Man, take this blunt." Then he cleared his throat. "Damn boo. I really need to go handle some shit right quick. Can we get up a lil' later."

"But Cam, I'm tryna see yo' sexy ass right now. I think this might help you make a decision."

Putting the phone on speaker, I sent a picture that I had Sita take of me earlier. It showed the tight, short ass red dress and high ass heels I was rocking. I knew how to reel him in.

"Shit, you lookin' good enough to eat mami. Why don't you just meet me on this side? By the time you get over here, I'll be done."

"Uh, I'm not drivin'."

"Why the hell you ain't drivin'? Ain't that the reason I bought you a damn whip?"

"Look babe, Sita dropped me off 'cause I just knew you'd meet me here."

"A'ight, tell me where you gon' be at and I'll be there in thirty minutes."

Spotting a Red Lobster, I told him, "I'll be at the Red Lobster. Hurry up baby."

"A'ight, I'm on my way."

With a satisfied smile, I sashayed across the street.

* * *

Sita and I were in her room talking when her cell phone rang.

"What's up?" She smiled all sly like, leaning back against the fluffy, pink pillows that were propped against the headboard of her bed.

Trying not to seem nosey, I pretended to be concentrating on what was on TV. I'd been telling her all about how jealous and psycho Rahz had been acting lately. I needed some advice. I'd been dealing with a couple other dudes, but Rahz was a big spender. I just didn't think his money was worth all the drama.

Rosita ended her call. "Okay, what was you sayin' now?"

"You know how sweet and generous I said Rahz can be, but lately, he's... different. I told you 'bout how he went off at the restaurant. I'm convinced that mufucka is really certified crazy. After that shit, I decided to go to his crib to talk, 'cause he kept on beggin'. He claimed he wasn't gonna do no shit like that again. Girl, I went to use the bathroom and when I came back he was going through my phone. I almost lost my damn mind. He's good as hell wit' numbers, so I know he memorized some of them. What the hell should I do about his ass? I mean, he does a lot for me. If it wasn't for him and Cam..."

"Fuck that shit. That nigga ain't right in the head. Cam does enough for you on his own for you to drop that nigga Rahz. Shit, I told yo' ass 'bout those Jamaican niggas, didn't I?" She shook her head at me.

"Sita, Cam ain't no better. He got too much damn baby mama drama. I get so sick of goin' back and forth with that bitch."

"Drop that hoe then," she told me as she lit a cigarette.

"Believe me cuz, I want to, but Cam won't let us fight. That shit's so damn aggravating."

"I feel you on that. Oh well, it's plenty niggas out there. What about Corion? He ain't all that fine, but he owns three clubs. Shit, milk him for that legal money. You know how to do it."

"Girl." Rolling my eyes, I spat, "That nigga's showin' signs of crazy too. I cut him off."

I'd met him a few weeks ago, but shit wasn't popping. I decided to not go any further with him

"Damn bih, what you doin' to these niggas? I might need to take a lesson from yo' ass." Sita laughed and slapped her thigh.

"I ain't doin' shit. I ain't even fuck Corion. He wasn't gon' get shit unless I got shit. I'm done though. He was a bit much."

Rosita gave me a nod of approval. "That's the shit I like to hear. Ma would be proud of you. She always told me, don't put out unless he put in."

That made me laugh. "Y'all some wild bitches."

"Girl, did I tell you 'bout last weekend?"

I shook my head.

"It was lit as fuck." She put her cigarette out in the ashtray.

"Yeah, didn't you and Cherrie go to New Orleans?"

"Uh huh and I met this nigga from New York. He was actin' so damn thirsty in the club and I was gettin' them free drinks. He was a'ight lookin' and he kept flossin' his stack of money. Cherrie was all up on his boy. You know we was schemin' and shit. Anyways, we ended up goin' wit' them to their hotel. These niggas were smokin', poppin' Xans and drinkin' Henney. I was tellin' that nigga to keep drinkin' so his dick can stay hard all night. Niggas got egos, so I had to stroke that shit a lil' bit. To make a long story short, I fucked the hell outta that nigga and put his drunk, high ass to sleep. He was snoring loud as hell. Man, I took all his money and his jewels and shit. After I got dressed, I got up outta that bitch. Then I called Cherrie. She was in the adjoining room with his boy. She'd already cleaned his ass out too. Them stupid mufuckas thought our names were April and Monique. We left that mufucka trippin' out over that shit. I bet they woke up and got a big ass shock. Fuck them niggas. Don't be flashin' yo' shit in my face, 'cause I'm a grimey ass bitch. Niggas ain't shit. Fuck 'em all."

Sita was too damn much. "Girl, you and Cherrie brave as hell. Ain't no way. What if those niggas killed y'all asses."

"Well, they didn't bitch. Plus, we only do that shit to niggas when we outta town. I gave him this good ass pussy, so he owed me. This pussy ain't free."

She was really rubbing off on me, because I agreed one hundred percent. "I'd be scared to do some shit like that. I ain't gon' lie."

"I was scared to do it the first time, but after a while, I ain't give a fuck no more. You gotta do it to a nigga that's drunk and high out of his mind. Then you gotta fuck him so damn good, he go to sleep right after. Don't be all cuddled up, 'cause you don't want him to wake up when you move. When he snorin' all nice and loud, you start goin' though his pockets for his stash. Most real ballers don't fuck wit' all that jewelry on, 'cause it gets in the way. More than likely, they'll take that shit off and put it on the nightstand. You just take a big ass bag so you can put all that shit in it. Make sure you wear some skimpy ass shit so it won't take you long to get dressed and get your ass outta there. Don't ever give a nigga yo' real name or tell him where you're from. Make up some bullshit right off the dome. You gotta lie yo' ass off and keep the lies straight. Make sure you're convincing. Men think we are innocent off top, so let him keep believing it."

"Do you ever feel... guilty?"

She looked at me like I'd lost my mind. "Hell nah. For what? Men are cold hearted ass snakes. They don't feel. They just move by instinct. Well, I learned to act and think just like them. If men are dogs, I'm a real bitch. I don't mind admitting it. I refuse to be the one who gets hurt, even if I have to do the hurting. You gotta control that love bullshit. Love yourself. Fuck a nigga."

Sita always talked with such conviction. Her mom had trained her well, or experience had made her that way one.

I'd always wondered, so I decided to ask. "Uh, what happened to make you feel the way you do about men?"

Was it just her mother, or something she'd been through? Maybe it was multiple things she'd been through to contribute to her discontent for the opposite sex.

Tears welled up in Sita's eyes. I'd never seen her look so vulnerable before.

"You ain't know all this, but that's 'cause I make it look so easy." As she sniffed, she continued. "Of course, you know my daddy was murdered. What you don't know is, he started molesting me when I was six. At first, I ain't know it was him doing that shit, because he'd either cover my face up with a pillow or a blanket. After a few years, he decided to take it further. He started actually fuckin' me when I was twelve and by the time I was fourteen, he stopped covering up my face. When I realized he was doing that shit to me, I was devastated. How could the man I loved with all my heart hurt me like that?" As she wiped her eyes, she kept talking, but her voice was lower. "He got me pregnant when I was fifteen. That's the only reason I finally told ma. At first, he threatened that if I told her, he'd do something to us both. That was after he tried to convince me that that was just what daddies do with their little girls. When my period stopped, I had to tell ma. There was no way I could have that baby. After I told her, he tried to convince my mama that I was a lil' hot ass hoe and was knocked up by a neighborhood boy. He claimed I was lyin' on him. My mom believed me, thankfully. She kicked him out and less than a month later he was found with a bullet wound to his head. Mama never admitted it, but I'm convinced she got one of our uncles to kill him. The murder was never solved and mama collected the life insurance. Shit, if my own daddy saw me as just a piece of pussy and didn't give a fuck about me, why should I expect some random nigga to? After that shit me and my mama lost faith in men. I got an abortion and life goes on."

Damn, that shit had me crying right along with my cousin. I decided to tell her about my own experiences with the men my mother slept with for money. Little did I know, but Sita and I had more in common than I thought.

Chapter 6

Florida

2013

The more I listened to Sita, the more I was pulled into her world. Her philosophy was really starting to become mine. My experience with Eddie had confirmed her theory that men weren't shit.

I'd gone with my better judgment and decided to take a breather from Rahz. It was the weekend and me and Sita were planning to hit up a hot spot. Cam had called and attempted to talk me out of going. Jealous ass.

Sighing heavily, he said, "Yo', I'on like the thought of niggas bein' all over you and shit."

"Don't be like that Cam. You know I ain't that bitch… and you go out when you want to. You can't lock me down, so it ain't no point in tryin'. Call me when you realize I ain't got no daddy."

After hanging up, I turned the phone off and made my way over to my walk-in closet. It was probably time for me to be done with Cam too and focus on myself. By that time, Sita and I had our own apartment together. We both had jobs to sustain us. Sita was working for the same telemarketing company as Gloria, but I decided to get a job as a waitress at a hookah lounge called Shadows. The tips were good, and I met plenty of niggas with money. However, after what I'd been through with Rahz and the drama with Cam's baby mama, I wasn't really trying to really fuck with anybody like that.

It was like once a nigga fucked, he thought he owned a bitch. I for one, didn't belong to anybody. How come a man always wanted to claim somebody, but didn't want anybody to claim them?

After taking a shower, getting dressed and doing my hair, I turned my phone back on. It immediately started to ring, and I thought it was Cam. Before I could send him to voicemail, I looked down and saw that it was Rahz calling. That didn't change the outcome. His ass was sent to voicemail.

There was a knock on my bedroom door. I knew it was Sita, so I told her to come in.

"You look fierce," she nodded in approval as she walked in my room.

Surveying her outfit, I saw that it was outrageously skimpy as usual. Her shorts were extra short, and her butt cheeks were hanging out. I was feeling like a goody two shoe ass square in my tight, white dress. It was short, but not that damn short.

"What the hell type of shirt is that?" I stared at the tiny piece of black, silky fabric that was the size of a wash cloth.

That shit barely covered her full C-cup breasts. To make it even worse, her titties spilled over the top and there were slits that almost showed her nipples. The black stiletto heel boots that she wore stopped at her upper thigh.

"This top cost more than yo' whole outfit. Now let's go."

Shaking my head at her, I grabbed my black Hermes bag and led the way. That was the night I met Duke. I'd already downed a bunch of shots of Patron and was feeling it when me and my cuz hit the dance floor. The club was packed to capacity, so people were shoulder to shoulder. That many black mufuckas in one spot had to be a fire hazard.

Sita was freaking some cute, light skinned dude. The dancefloor was so damn tight, I could barely move. That shit didn't stop Sita from going down to the floor as she gyrated and twerked her ass. My bitch was out there, but I couldn't hate. She was doing her "thang" and I was all for it.

When I looked to my left there was a group of thirsty ass looking niggas hovering around Sita like a pack of wolves. Shaking my head, I just kept on swaying to the music. All of a sudden, I felt someone tap me on the shoulder. When I turned around, I was face to face with a caramel colored nigga with sexy, captivating, dark brown eyes. As much as I tried not to, I couldn't help but stare. Usually I didn't go for anything other than dark skinned men, but that mufucka was an exception.

I turned around and that nigga started gyrating against my ass like we'd just spent the damn night together. Damn. He was so damn fine, I threw it back at him like I wanted that D. Catching

Sita's eye, I noticed that she was smiling slyly at me. Then she winked as she put her leg around some nigga's waist. She was twerking and humping the hell out of dude. He didn't know what to do and the lustful look in his eyes was obvious.

That's when the DJ started playing some old school reggae. I could feel that nigga's hard dick pressed against my back as I wined into him. His hands were on my waist, holding on for dear life as I worked it out on him. He pulled me closer into his body as I sang along, "No, no, no... You don't love me, and I know now."

His breath was on my ear, causing chills to spread all over my entire anatomy.

"Mmm... you something else ma," he whispered. "I wanna see you again after tonight. No games."

That nigga's voice was deep and almost hypnotizing. His accent sounded like he was from up north or something. Suddenly, Sita pulled me away from him. That shit pissed me off so bad, I was cursing up something as she dragged me toward the restroom.

"Damn bitch. What the fuck? Why the hell you pull me away from that fine, good smelling mufucka? This shit better be good." My arms were across my chest as I stared at her.

She didn't say a word as she applied more lips gloss to her already moist lips. Pretending to be fixing her perfect, red hair, she didn't acknowledge what I'd said. Not one hair was out of place, and I was starting to grow impatient.

"What if I don't see him again?"

"You will... shut up bih..." she told me through clenched teeth.

The other chicks left the restroom and she starting to talk fast as hell. "His name is Duke bitch. He's big time for fuckin' real. I ain't playin' when I say you was just grindin' all over a big fish. He's makin' more money than Cam and Rahz combined. That mufucka got a mini-mansion in Roychester Estates and he drives a silver Hummer amongst many other hot ass whips."

Some more chicks walked in and Sita lowered her voice. "You done hit the fuckin' jackpot, so don't fuck that shit up worryin' 'bout them other niggas. And you will see him again. He's on yo' ass and he'll hunt yo' sexy ass down if he wants you bad enough."

How did that hoe know everything about everybody? She was definitely on it when it came to who had the most money in Miami. Damn, did she have a radar for that shit?

"Well, he got an accent like he's from up north or something. Where's he from?"

"I don't know for sure, but I know he lived in Maryland for a while. B-more, I think."

With a nod, I headed toward the door. "Well, let's go then bitch. Why the hell did you pull me away from him, you could've told me about that shit later."

I was trying to catch a big fish.

"Sorry cuz. I was just excited and shit."

We headed back to the dancefloor as I shook my head. Why the fuck was she excited when that nigga was into me?

By the end of the night Duke had sniffed me out again. We were on the way back to Sita's black 2011 Maxima when he crept up behind me.

"Yo' ma, I ain't get yo' name."

"I didn't give it, but what's yours?"

"Duke," he stuck his hand out for me to shake.

"I'm Xa."

He kissed my hand and stared down at me.

"Mmm, I'm feelin' your feistiness."

Damn, he was tall just like I liked.

His eyes narrowed as they drifted in Sita's direction. "Do I know you? You look hella familiar."

"We never officially met, but I kicked it wit' yo' homeboy Vince a while back."

"Oh okay. You the red head shawty he showed me the picture of."

Smiling, she nodded. "Yeah, I'm Sita. Xa's my cousin."

"Okay, okay." His focus was back on me.

"Miss Xa... you fuckin' gorgeous as hell. It was no way I was gon' let you get away tonight."

Damn, I was blushing, but trying to keep it cool and shit.

Smiling hard, he revealed deep dimples.

"Where yo' phone at ma?"

Reaching in my bag, I fished it out.

"Make sure you program my number and use it too." His voice was bossy, but sexy.

"Okay," I simply told him.

After I programmed his number, he asked me. "So, you got a man?"

"Nah, I'on have that problem."

"Psycho baby daddy, or daddies?"

"No kids, how 'bout you?"

"I'm single as hell, but I got a daughter. No baby mama drama though. She lives in Maryland and she got her own life. I'on interfere."

By that time, Sita had sauntered off to the car. I gave him my number and then he started walking with me. After I was safely buckled up, we said our goodbyes and he proceeded to his own vehicle.

"Let's sit here for a minute. I wanna see what that nigga's pushin'," I said.

"He probably drivin' his silver Hummer."

Sita lit a stinking ass Newport and I lowered the window. I hated how those shits smelled.

"I'on see no Hummer out here other than that yellow one."

"It's a huge ass parking lot Xa."

With my eyes still on him, I watched him get in a charcoal gray Bentley. Damn, now that shit impressed me. He had two niggas with him that were waiting in the car. That nigga was driving, but I wondered if that shit was his. It wasn't like he couldn't be driving somebody else's shit. If it was his, I'd hit the jackpot for real. Cha ching!

* * *

Later that week, I was on pins and needles waiting for Duke to call me. Yeah, I had his number, but I didn't want to be the one to call first. I didn't want him to think I was sweating his ass. Me and Sita were decked out in some hot ass two-piece bathing suits, chilling on the beach. My phone was right by my side and I kept right on checking that shit. The only calls I had were from Rahz and Cam, but I didn't want to talk to either of them.

"Why you keep on checkin' yo' phone?" Sita sucked her teeth as she asked.

Her eyes were on some niggas who were sitting not too far from us. They were sitting with some white bitches, so I didn't know why she was clocking them.

"That nigga Duke ain't called me yet. He pushin' a damn Hummer and a Bentley. That nigga can't be single as hell like he said. I can guarantee some bitch done snatched that up," I admitted.

"He'll call you and if he got a bitch or not, it don't fuckin' matter. Why you care? He got enough money to go 'round." Sita shook her head like I was losing it. "That nigga wants you. He just tryna play hard and shit like he ain't impressed. Just like you. You got my blood in you though, so you good. You a diva bitch, so don't you ever doubt a nigga wants you."

A few hours later we headed to the crib. It was after nine and I wanted to smoke some gas and have a strong ass drink. The first thing we both did was take a shower and then we met up in the kitchen. We both wanted something to drink on.

"I got a bottle of Ace that Dajaun gave me," Sita said opening the fridge.

Yeah, she'd already moved on from Rob. She'd filled me in that he was on some violent shit. One night she popped off at the mouth and he choked her out. After that, she was done with his ass. According to her, for once, money wasn't enough.

I grabbed the champagne glasses.

It was a boring ass Thursday night and we were both trying to make the best of it. It was my day off and Sita had quit her job. I was trying to help her get on where I was. She'd often complained about the monotony of working at a call center and the annoying ass people on the other line. In the meantime, her mother and her niggas made sure her bills were paid.

Being that I was once again on my own financially, I didn't have the luxury of quitting my job. As much as I loved a man helping me out, I didn't want to rely on that. One other lesson I had learned was just how unreliable a nigga was.

"It's a boring ass Thursday night. Might as well get drunk."

She filled both our glasses and then we clinked them together as if we were toasting.

"He gon' call you."

"It don't really matter. It's other suckas out there."

By my second glass, I was about to say fuck Duke and call Cam for some dick. Then, my cell phone started to vibrate on the end table. It was Duke's fine ass. Finally. Sita gave me an anxious look as I answered.

"Hello."

"Sup ma?"

"Ain't shit. Just chillin', drinkin' some Ace with my cuz."

"Some Ace? Damn, y'all big ballin'."

With a laugh, I asked him, "So, what's goin' on wit' you?"

"On my way to the crib. I just left the mall. Had to get me some kicks and shit. I mean, I gotta keep myself up if I wanna get wit' a fine ass woman like you."

That lop-sided grin of his was etched in my memory.

"Hmm, we'll see…"

"Look, I ain't gon' beat around the bush. That just ain't me. I'm upfront wit' shit. I wasn't spittin' game to you. I was serious when I said I want to see you again. Let me take you out and show you a good time. You know, make yo' life lit."

With a smile, I told him, "You probably got a bench full of bitches. Why me?"

"Shit, why not you?"

That was a good ass question.

We talked for hours and decided to go out that Saturday. The next couple days flew by and I was so psyched about seeing Duke. We'd been talking on the phone non-stop. Shit, I was feeling that fine, rich muthafucka.

At around seven o' clock, he was ringing the doorbell and I wasn't quite ready. A bitch was trying to lay my edges. I'd gotten a nice ass sew in, because Miami's humidity was bad on my natural hair.

"Go get the door Sita!" I yelled out.

In ten minutes, I was ready. Checking myself out in the full-length mirror, I couldn't help but approve. My hair was slayed, face was beat, brows on fleek and lashes were looking exotic. Hopefully Duke would approve of the sexy ass white bandage dress that was glued to my curves.

When I walked in the front, his eyes widened, and his jaw dropped.

"Damn, you killin' that fuckin' dress. Mmm." Shaking his head, he closed the distance between us and handed me a dozen red roses.

"Thank you." I couldn't help but blush.

Sita looked impressed as she watched our exchange. "Well, y'all have fun."

She left the room and gave us some privacy.

Pulling me into his fragrant body, I took in the scent of his cologne. My head started swimming. I put the flowers in a vase and we headed to his car. He was driving the Bentley and I knew then that it was his. That nigga was such a gentleman. Not only did he open my car door, but he held my hand to help me get in.

In a short amount of time he opened up and told me a lot of shit about his life. He filled me in that he was originally from Washington DC, but moved to Baltimore with his mother when he was ten. By that time his father was well into a life sentence for murder.

By the age of sixteen, he was out of control. He ended up joining a gang and started slinging heroin, and cocaine. When he was seventeen he caught a gun charge. He did a year and a half and then moved to Miami for a change of scenery.

He and his right-hand man Semaj had the streets locked down when it came to the drug game. They sold it all from heroin to pills. Those niggas were moving real weight and making some major coins. Not only that, but they owned their own recording studio. They charged niggas for studio time and beats. Then he added that they also bred pit bulls, and bull mastiffs.

Our first date was perfect, I had to admit. We had a fancy ass dinner on a yacht. They were playing live jazz and all. That shit was sophisticated as hell. Duke even wore a money green Italian three-piece suit and some tan Red Bottom gators. He was looking good enough to eat.

"How's your food?" He asked.

"Delicious."

I'd ordered the herb crusted salmon with asparagus and cream potatoes. He had the blackened bass with mixed vegetables, and lobster mac and cheese.

Once we were done eating, he grabbed my hand and led me to the dance floor. Although he seemed to be an unrefined thug when I met him, now I saw a different side of him. He held me close and I almost melted into the floor as we glided to the music. Damn, all I'd ever done was grind and twerk on a nigga. That was something different.

By twelve, we both were toasted off that champagne we drunk. When we got in his car, he lit up a spliff, hit it and passed it to me. Damn, that shit was right on time. We talked some more, but I kept it vague about my past. He didn't need to know everything about me just yet. Besides, I really had nothing to tell.

Duke's phone rung and he answered it with an anxious look on his face.

"What's up Ro?"

After a long pause, he let out a sigh. "Man, shit. A'ight. I'll be there in fifteen."

He hung up and looked over at me. "I'm sorry shawt. I gotta make a pit stop 'fore I take you home."

Wow, I was impressed. That nigga wasn't even trying to get any pussy. His plan was to take me home.

"A'ight." I nodded and looked out of the window as he drove.

He turned the radio up and a song by Drake blared from the speakers. I bobbed my head and noticed that he was staring at me.

"What?" There was something about the way he was looking at me that turned me on.

"You got me tempted to not take you home. You lookin' all good, but I'm gon' be a gentleman. I got plans for you and I ain't tryna rush shit. I really enjoyed spendin' time wit' you though."

"And I enjoyed spendin' time wit' you too."

He nodded. "That's good. So, I'll see you again, right beautiful?"

"Yes."

We pulled up to what looked like a warehouse. It was surrounded by other warehouses, but there was only one other car parked outside. That was a sign that none of the other businesses in the vicinity were open. Why the fuck were we there?

"You wait out here baby girl. I'll be right back." After kissing my cheek, he got out of the car.

Was I going to be safe out there? Shit, it was dark as hell.

"Will you be long?"

"Nah, you good. I promise."

"Okay."

He walked off and I pulled out my phone to call Sita. She'd already texted asking me if I was sucking that nigga's dick yet. I texted her back and told her I wasn't her. She sent me the laughing emoji back.

"Girl, how's yo' date goin'?" She asked.

"Good. We had so much fun and I was surprised that we actually didn't do no hood shit. That nigga acts like a rich nigga. He ain't nothing like Cam and Rahz."

"I told you."

There was loud music in the background, so I figured she was out and shit.

"What you doin'?"

"At a house party wit' Cherrie. This mufuckin' house is big as shit. It's an indoor pool in here and all. This shit is lit."

"Sounds fun." It was a good thing that I'd have the crib to myself to chill for a while.

"I'm lookin' for a nigga to set up tonight bitch. Fuck fun. I need some money?"

"Set up?"

"Oh my god, you so naïve. We'll talk about it later. I gotta go. I see a potential. Bye cuz."

Shaking my head, I hung up and looked around. An eerie feeling rushed over me as I relit the blunt. Damn, I hoped he'd hurry the fuck up. Then the sound of a gun shot rang out and filled the silence of the night.

Less than ten seconds later, I saw Duke rushing toward the car. He got in without saying a word and drove off. Did he just shoot somebody while I was waiting in the damn car? Had that nigga made me an accessory to a murder I knew nothing about on our first damn date? What the fuck? Our perfect date had gone left.

Since he wasn't volunteering any information, I asked. "What just happened?"

"Nothing." He turned the music up, which was a sign that he wasn't trying to tell me shit.

"Umm, I heard a gunshot Duke."

"My business is my business shawt. What you don't know won't hurt you."

"For real? So, the fact that what you just did could fall back on me makes it not my business? If you killed somebody and I was on the fuckin' car wit' you, that makes me an accessory. What if shit would've gotten out of control and I got shot."

"I'd never let nothing happen to you and that shit comes wit' the territory when you fuck wit' a nigga like me."

"Well, I personally don't wanna deal wit' what comes wit' the territory. Do what the fuck you want. You a grown ass man, but don't involve me in that shit. You could've took me home and then handled that."

"You're right." He let out a sigh and rubbed his chin thoughtfully. "Next time I'll do shit different shawt."

Shit, the way I was feeling, there may not be a next time. Fuck that shit.

Chapter 7

Atlanta

2017

Although I was visiting to spend time with my mom, she was always at work. I was thinking she'd be able to take some time off, but she was a head cashier and they claimed they needed her. So, my bored ass decided to go out. Ma had promised we'd spend some time together the next day, since it was her day off. My plan was to leave the day after that.

After a hot shower, I got dressed and looked up the address for the Velvet Rope. It was about twenty minutes away from my mom's house. The reviews said it was off the hook. Shit, I was going by myself. It wasn't like I was cool with Chloe anymore and Alicia was on lock down.

Jumping in my car, I looked at myself in my rearview mirror. Making sure that my nose was clean, and my makeup was flawless, I drove away once I was sure I was good. The club was easy to find since I'd put the address in my GPS.

The spot was packed, and I drove around for ten minutes looking for an empty parking space. There were some hot ass whips out there, so I knew some money makers were up in the club. Almost every other vehicle was suited up with rims, body kits, expensive tint and the whole nine.

As I stepped out of the car, I wondered if I was dressed too damn slutty. My short dress barely covered my ass and I pulled it down hoping it wouldn't ride my thighs too bad all night. The five carat diamond earrings that Cam had given me glistened in the moonlight. They were one gift that I kept near and dear.

Walking in the club, it felt like all eyes were on me. Well, they should've been, because I was looking like a full-course dinner, fuck a damn snack. I was hoping to find somebody who had some weed. The entire time I'd been in Atlanta, I hadn't smoked shit.

My first stop was the bar, and that shit was crowded as hell. It took me nearly fifteen minutes just to order my drink. Right as I was about to pay for my Hennessey and Coke, I heard a raspy voice say, "I got that."

He passed the bartender a twenty-dollar bill, but his eyes were stuck on me.

"What's your name sexy?"

Unfortunately, I couldn't say the same for him, because he was far from sexy. He was brown skinned, skinny as hell with bug eyes and huge, black lips. Those shits looked like that nigga smoked a carton of cigarettes a day. Something told me not to let him pay for my drink, but I did. I just hoped he wouldn't be stalking me all night.

"I'm Nesha and thank you," I said, giving him a fake name.

"I'm Shank."

The bartender gave him his change as I sipped the drink.

"Well, thank you, Shank."

As I started to walk off, he asked me, "So, you here by yourself?"

"Nah, I'm wit' my girls. They on the dancefloor." That was another lie because I didn't want him to think I was vulnerable and alone.

"Okay, well, I hope you save a dance for me."

Flashing a fake smile, I told him, "I will," and sauntered off.

Thankfully, he didn't keep on harassing me. After I finished my drink off, I threw the empty cup in the trash and headed for the dancefloor. As I shook my ass to the beat of Savage 21's "Flexing on My Ex," I felt somebody grab hold of my waist.

When I looked back, I saw that nigga Shank. Rolling my eyes, I tried to pull away from him, but some other nigga came up and started dancing in front of me. Next thing I knew, those niggas had me in a sandwich. They were both sweaty and obviously drunk. The looks they kept sharing let me know that they were in cahoots and trying to tag team me. Those niggas were groping my ass and shit and I was about to throat punch one of those fools. The only thing was, I couldn't move my damn arms.

"Move!" I screamed, pushing, trying to get away from their grasp.

Their perspiration dripped onto my face and I could smell the alcohol, cigarettes and weed that laced their breath. The stench was horrific as hell. A bitch almost threw the fuck up.

"Get the fuck off me!" I attempted to shove the one in front of me, so I could get away, but he wouldn't budge.

"Chill babe, we just wanna dance wit' yo' fine ass. Plus, my nigga bought you a drink."

"Man, fuck that drink." It wasn't like I'd asked that nigga for that shit.

Shank held on to me tightly as he grinded harder into my ass. I wanted to really go off when I felt his hand travel up my inner thigh.

"If you don't get yo' fuckin' hands off me!" With all my might, I tried to escape, but it was to no avail. Each time I tried to hit one of those niggas, they squashed me between them harder, so I couldn't move.

Suddenly, I felt myself being yanked away from the two, intoxicated beasts. I couldn't see who had rescued me, because it had happened so fast. When he finally let me go, I said, "Thanks," and looked back.

"Oh, it's you."

"Oh, it's me? Damn, you ungrateful as hell. Those niggas were 'bout to take the pussy right there on the dancefloor. Unless you wanted that shit." He shook his head.

"I didn't need yo' help."

"It ain't look that way to me."

"Well, I didn't."

"Man, as much as I still want you... you got me wantin' to say fuck that shit."

"Well, why don't you?" There was a sarcastic smirk on my face.

"I can't." His eyes stayed on mine like he was trying to see if I felt anything for him.

"I don't know why. Y'en give a fuck when you had me."

He grabbed me and pulled me into his solid body. "I saw you in a fucked up ass position, so I helped you. I've always been yo' protector. I ain't gon' stop now 'cause I fucked up what we had five years ago. This ain't the time or the place to talk about that, but I want you to know that I ain't gon' give up on you. I'll leave you alone...for now."

He let me go and walked away. Part of me wanted to follow him, but I didn't. As much as I wanted that familiar feeling of security with Eddie, that shit wasn't real. I was no longer in a partying mood, so I left the club. Walking slowly to my car, I heard a voice ask, "You leavin' already shawty?"

I didn't respond.

"Damn, it must be wack as fuck in there," he said.

After I got in my car, I drove off with all types of thoughts fogging my mind. Did I still love Eddie? Did I ever stop?

* * *

Miami
2013

Two weeks had passed since my date with Duke. At first, I ruled out fucking with him, but Sita had helped change my mind.

"Girl, it ain't like that nigga involved you in that shit physically. Fuck it. He had to handle his business. You checked him and so it's all good. Don't fuck it up, 'cause you ain't 'bout that life bitch. You better harden up a lil' bit. Ain't nobody tellin' you to be some queen pin, or start poppin' niggas for him, but damn. Get over that shit and get that nigga's bank."

So, over the past two weeks, we went out a few more times. Rahz had finally stopped calling, but not Cam. I guess because he gave me a car, he felt like I was obligated to him. As far as I was concerned, he could have it back if he was going to hold that shit over my head.

The last time we were together, his stupid ass baby mama popped up talking shit again. Of course, he wouldn't let me bust that in the mouth bitch like I really wanted to. As much as I wanted to keep fucking with Cam, that shit was getting tired. I was hoping to catch that bitch Ebony by her damn self. Bet she wouldn't be running her old funky ass mouth then.

Early one Friday morning, my phone rang at six forty-five. Before answering, I cleared the frog from my throat.

'Hello," I said, hoping I didn't sound like a man.

"Good morning sunshine," Duke's voice serenaded my eardrum.

"Good morning handsome. Uh, do you know how early it is?"

Letting out a chuckle, he said, "I know, but I wanna see yo' pretty face. How 'bout I come scoop you at 'bout ten."

"Ten a.m., or p.m.?"

"C'mon boo, a.m. I can't wait. I got something planned for us, so be ready. A'ight?"

He sounded so confident that I'd go. Despite the fact that I wasn't a morning person, I couldn't help but smile. If only he knew that I had plans for him too, but he probably wouldn't like mine.

After our goodbyes, I ended the call. It wasn't quite seven yet, so I set my alarm and snuggled back under the covers. Anxious to see what Duke had up his sleeve, I couldn't go back to sleep. I probably drifted off ten minutes before the alarm went off.

Jumping up, I went ahead and took a shower. I could hear Sita moving around and the smell of something cooking. Sita was always up early as hell. Damn, that shower had given me life. I loved the six massage settings on the shower head. That was for more reasons than one.

After my shower, I threw on a bathrobe and headed to the kitchen. Sita had brewed some coffee and had threw down on breakfast. There were blueberry and banana nut muffins, scrambled cheese eggs, grits and bacon. There was also a platter of fresh pineapples, strawberries, honey dew melon and grapes.

"Eat somethin' cuz," she greeted me with a wide grin.

"We havin' company?" There was a lot of food, and so I was curious.

"No. I just felt like cookin' a big breakfast."

That bitch was in a good mood like she'd gotten some banging ass dick the night before. Either that, or a nigga had bought her something expensive.

"Mmm, you must've got yo' back broken in last night bitch," I teased as I fixed my plate.

"Yeah, I guess you can say that nigga Dajuan put it down."

Hmm, she'd been seeing him a lot lately and he was the only nigga I ever heard her talk about. Cuz must've been feeling him more than she'd admit. I wasn't going to call her out though. If it was me, I wouldn't hear the end of that shit.

Sticking her hand out, she squealed, "And he bought me this ring bitch! It's three and a half carats." The rock shined and gleamed in the light.

"It's hot cuz. Umm, did ya'll get...?"

"Bitch bye. Hell nah we ain't get engaged." That smile was turned upside down.

"Damn bitch, my bad. Thanks for the breakfast crazy."

"You're welcome, but why the hell you up so early? You usually sleep past twelve."

"Duke's pickin' me up for an early date girl. He called me at six somethin' talkin' 'bout he made plans."

Rolling my eyes, I pretended to be annoyed.

"Oh okay, I feel that. Don't fuck that up Xa for real. Milk him for all he's worth. Shit, I wish I was the one that nigga had pushed up on."

Did I see a twitch of envy in her eyes?

"Okay, coach," I joked trying not to think my cousin would be jealous of me.

It was silent after that and we finished eating without saying much.

"I'm gonna go get dressed. I gotta get my hair done. I got a date tonight too bitch."

"Wit' Dajuan."

"Nah, his name's Landon."

With that said, she left the kitchen and didn't give me any more details on this new dude. Was she really in her feelings about Duke? If she wanted him so bad, why didn't she just tell me before I started fucking with him?

* * *

Me and Duke went out for breakfast and I wolfed down some chicken and waffles. He had shrimp and grits, so it wasn't hard to tell that he loved seafood. As usual, our conversation flowed as we sipped on mimosas. Damn, I enjoyed each of our dates as it was the first.

"Mmm... you know it's hard to keep bein' a gentleman, right?"

His hand was on the small of my back as he led me to his silver Beemer. Yes honey, he had a fleet of hot ass whips.

"Whatever do you mean?" I asked in an exaggerated southern accent, pretending to clutch my pearls.

He laughed. "You know what I mean, and I'm sure it's worth the wait."

Something told me that we wouldn't be waiting much longer. After we stopped at an African Art gallery for him to pick up an oil painting, we went to a luxurious clothing boutique. Not only were the clothes expensive as hell, but everything was so fashion forward. The shoes were too die for, and everything was a high-end brand.

"Why are we here?"

Duke greeted the lady behind the counter.

"Hey Grace."

She looked up at him and smiled pleasantly.

"How're you Duke?"

"Couldn't be better."

He introduced me as his girl and then told me to get whatever I wanted. Once I had a bunch of shit on the counter, I watched him pay for it with a black card. Wow, the total was seven thousand dollars and he didn't even flinch. I hadn't even given that nigga any pussy yet.

When we left the boutique, it was a little after five o' clock.

"You hungry again yet?"

"Are you?"

He chuckled. "A little."

We ended up at Benihana's and I loved Japanese food. After hibachi filet mignon, rice, veggies and Saki, it was on to a comedy show downtown. That shit was hilarious, and my side was hurting by the time we left.

"So, you wanna go home or..."

"I wanna go home wit' you."

That shit made a sly smile spread across his lips. It was time to sample that dick. Damn, I was horny and hoped that shit was good.

* * *

"So, you just knew you was gonna get some tonight, huh?"

Duke had his sprawling, four-bedroom, five and a half bath home decked out for romance. Rose petals led a path from the front door to the master bathroom, which was on the second floor. There were also rose petals on the bed in the shape of a heart. A bottle of champagne was on the nightstand along with whip cream, chocolate sauce, strawberries and pineapples.

"Well..." He grinned cockily. "Get comfy ma. I'm 'bout to go grab a bucket of ice for the champagne. As a matter of fact, fuck that, get naked."

Shaking my head, I watched his fine ass walk away. When he came back, he couldn't help but lick his lips and rub his hands together hungrily. I was butt ass naked, except for my high heels. It was a good thing I opted not to wear underwear.

I'd also just gotten a fresh Brazilian wax a couple day earlier.

"Wow, yo' body is on ten." His eyes dropped between my thighs. "And that pussy is so fuckin' fat. I'm ready to taste it."

He poured us both some Ace, since he thought I liked it. I did, but I couldn't afford that shit. After he took a sip, he kissed me deeply, and dropped down to his knees. I continued to drink as his lips crept up my calf to my thigh.

"Mmm..." Closing my eyes, I enjoyed the tingles that were traveling up and down my spine.

Arching my back, I spread my legs wider, putting my glass on the nightstand.

"Scoot up some," Duke directed, looking up at me with those captivating ass eyes.

I scooted to the edge of the bed and he cupped my ass cheeks in his strong hands. After covering my pussy in whip cream, he grabbed a strawberry. He pushed the strawberry inside of me. Then he dipped his head down and went in on a bitch's pussy. My clit was pulsating, and my walls were vibrating as he sucked the pure life out of my body along with that strawberry.

"Ohhh... shit... damn..." My eyes were glued to him, watching as he stared up at me, devouring my pussy along with my soul.

Duke added some chocolate syrup, lapped it up and then placed a pineapple inside of me. Slowly, he sucked it out and I felt the warmth of his tongue replace it.

Shit, I couldn't help but grind and rotate my hips as he traveled from my pussy to the crack of my ass. He made his way back to my clit and started humming as he assaulted that shit with his tongue. He kept sucking, and slurping and making loud ass smacking noises.

Then he slid his pointer and middle fingers deep inside of me. Pussy juice started to trickle down to the crack of my ass, and he got even more into it. Damn, that nigga had his whole face buried in my pussy. He was making circles and figure eights with his tongue, giving me life and then taking it over and over again.

"Ahhhh... oh myyy... fuckin'..." The head was so good, I couldn't even form a coherent sentence. My mouth was wide open the entire time, so my tongue was dry as shit.

"Mmm... mmm... mmm..." It sounded like he was smacking on a damn five-star meal.

Grabbing his head, I knew I was about to cum so hard it might just blow his damn head off.

"Fuck... ahhh... shit... ohhh... Duke... damn... mmm... argghhh... fuck! That shit feels so fuckin' good! Damn... nigga... eat that pussy... fuck!"

Hot tears rushed to the surface as I humped that nigga's face like I was riding his dick. That nut was just what I needed, and it rushed over me like the strongest drug in the word traveling through my veins. It was a syrupy warm feeling that enveloped my entire anatomy like a cocoon. As my legs shook, I still had that nigga's head in a vice grip.

His ass just kept right on licking and then started slurping my clit in and out of his mouth gently. Fuck... there it was... again. That warm feeling rushed down to my abdomen and spread down to the depths of my pussy. Ohhh, it was like I was cuming inside and out and my juices gushed out full force. He licked his fingers clean as he stared at me in longing.

"Damn ma, you taste so good. That pussy's tight too. That's good... but I hope you can take all this meat."

He pulled that dick out and I literally lost my breath. It was the thickest, longest dick I'd ever seen in my life. The main vein was huge and stuck out so far, it was like I could see that shit throbbing with each heartbeat. Oh shit... I thought Rahz had a big ass dick. That nigga Duke's shit looked like a damn elephant trunk. What the fuck? My walls were about to be pulverized to a pulp. No wonder he ate my pussy like that. My shit would have to be super wet to take that damn monster.

"Don't worry." He must've read my facial expression. "I know how to use it ma. I won't hurt it. I promise."

With my eyes glued to that shit, I watched him slide on a Trojan XL that barely covered it. Damn, I hoped it would stay on. His dick swung between his thick, muscular thighs as he positioned himself over me. My ass was still hanging off the bed as his hands spread my thighs apart.

With his fingers, he stirred my pussy up some more, causing wet sounds to fill the room.

"Mmm ma," he groaned. "Can't wait to feel those walls grippin' my dick."

Removing his fingers, he licked them. Then he reached down, grabbed his dick and started sliding it up and down the length of my slippery pussy. Once he was done teasing, he slid toward my entrance and slowly made his way in.

"Ahhh..." Squeezing my eyes closed, I tried to ignore the sharp, searing pain of the pressure his huge dick was putting on my walls.

"You okay?" He looked down at me and stopped.

All I wanted to know was, did he have that whole mufucka inside of me? I was wet though and once he had me loosened, my pussy was popping on that dick.

"Fuck!" Staring up at him in awe, I was amazed at how quickly he touched my G-spot.

That nigga had my pussy so wide open, I never knew I could nut from penetration so fast. He held on to my ass cheeks and squeezed as he dug inside of me with the moves of a male stripper. That nigga could work that back and he knew what to do with that anaconda.

"Shit... mmm... Xa... I wanna take this condom off so bad ma... Yo' pussy so fuckin' fye!"

"No... don't take it off... Not this time..." I threw in to make him think it may be a chance. Damn, that nigga was fucking up the mood with that bullshit.

Turning me over, he slapped my ass cheeks before sliding his length deep inside me. That time it didn't really hurt, but damn if I didn't feel that shit.

"Ohh... ohhhh...." The sound of my ass slapping into his pelvis was the only music we needed.

My pussy was so damn juicy, it sounded like that nigga was cooking soul food up in that bitch. You'd think he was stirring up mac and cheese, potato salad and banana pudding. It smelled like some banging ass sex was going on up in there. Good thing a bitch had good hygiene and he did too.

His finger was teasing the crack of my ass and I wrapped my legs around his waist, pulling him in deeper as an orgasm shook me again.

"Fuck Duke... shit..."

His body jerked and his grip on my hips tightened. Staring down at me, he bit down on his bottom lip and shook his head in amazement.

"ARGGGHHHH... damn... Xa... work that pussy on that dick!"

That nigga kept right on stroking like he was trying to come even harder than he already was. His dick pulsated inside of me and then he slowly pulled it out. My eyes were glued to it, making sure the condom was still intact. With all that wild shit we were doing, thankfully, it was.

He walked off to flush the condom and then came back with a hot soapy wash cloth to clean me off. Once I was straight, he left the room and then returned to join me in bed. We laid up butt naked and talked until the sun peeked through the blinds.

Before I knew it, that nigga's huge dick was up in me again. That time, I rode him to sleep, knowing that soon, my plan to get that bank would be in full force.

Chapter 8

Miami

2014

"Damn, that nigga's spoilin' you bitch," Sita spat as she took in the array of roses and chocolates that Duke had delivered to me for Valentine's Day.

Another bunch of packages came with outfits and shoes. Then there was another delivery of designer handbags. I knew that nigga had spent a fortune. He'd pulled out all the stops and we'd only been dealing with each other for six months. The only thing was, he couldn't spend Valentine's Day with me. Apparently, he was out of town handling some business. Initially, he was supposed to be back in town, but he claimed some shit came up and he'd be back on the sixteenth.

Yeah, it was something fishy about his vague ass explanation, but I didn't question it. Long as he was spending those funds, I was okay. That was what I was trying to convince myself anyway. Deep down inside, the thought of him spending Valentine's Day with somebody else kind of got to me.

"You fallin' in love wit' him, ain't you?" Sita's voice didn't sound as judgmental as I thought it would.

"No... I'm not. It is what it is. He spends money on me. That's what I love."

"Okay," she said skeptically. "If you say so."

"Shut up Sita, damn. I care about him, yes. I don't really wanna deal wit'a lotta niggas. Duke got enough money. I try not to feel anything for him, but I just do." My confusion was at an all-time high.

I was still seeing Cam occasionally, but Rahz was history. I'd changed my number and all, so he'd stop blowing my phone up. There was no way I'd ever deal with his ass again.

"You think you the only one Xavia?"

"No, but..."

She cut me off. "Good, 'cause you know you ain't. Why limit yourself to just him 'cause he got enough money? You sound crazy as hell. A nigga like Duke can afford to entertain a lotta bitches. You'll be stupid to think you're the only one."

"I ain't stupid enough to think I'm the only one Sita. You've never heard me say that shit. Don't play me. I'd never put anything past Duke or any other nigga. Now, like I said, I'm not in love with him, but don't try to tell me how to feel."

At that point, I was angry. She was getting on my nerves always being in my business.

Later that evening, Duke called.

"I wish you were here," I whined thinking about how good that nigga could eat some pussy.

"Me too. Hold on baby."

Straining my ears, I tried to hear what was going on in the back ground.

There were muffled voices, but I couldn't make out anything.

"I'm back," he said a few seconds later. "Look, I'm gonna have you call you back in a few. Some shit came up baby."

"We haven't even been on the phone for five damn minutes Duke."

"I'm in the middle of something ma. I'll call you back," he told me in a stern voice.

"Okay, tell Semaj, I said what's up."

"Don't sound like that. You know you my baby girl. I'm gon' make it up to you when I touch down in a couple days. A'ight."

"A'ight." With a sigh, I pressed the end button.

Sita was gone for the night and I was feeling restless. Instead of moping around the house, I decided to call this chick named Cherrie that me and Sita were cool with.

"What's up for the night girl?"

"Hey Xa. I was 'bout to hit up a spot by myself."

"I feel you on that shit. It's whatever though. I need to get out."

"It's Valentine's Day. I thought you'd be out with Duke or something."

"Nah, he's outta town handlin' some business and shit."

"Okay, I'll come pick you up in 'bout an hour. Be ready. I know how slow yo' ass can be."

We both laughed. "I'll be ready."

"Okay, later girl."

"Later."

I'd just finished getting dressed when the doorbell rang. Cherrie was standing there with two Coronas in her hand.

"I figured we'd get the party started here first bih. Shit, I'm ready to get fucked up." After giving me one of the beers, she held up a rolled blunt.

We sat down on the sofa and chatted as we smoked and sipped. She filled me in that she wasn't fucking with anybody like that, so Valentine's Day was just another day to her. Once we were buzzing, we headed to her gold Camry.

She was decked out in an extra short, tight black Gucci dress with silver G's all over it. Her silver high heeled sandals looked like stripper shoes. That was fitting being that Cherrie was a stripper. I was simply wearing a pair of dark blue True Religion jeans, but they looked painted on. My top was low cut and showed my pierced belly button.

"Where we goin'?" I asked as I put on my seat belt.

"A new sports bar called Rucker's. It's a hot spot. We can get some drinks and chill."

"Good." Leaning back in my seat, I added, "Because I ain't in the mood for no club."

"Me either, shit. I'm just tryna push up on some niggas and get some free drinks."

We both agreed on that.

Cherrie and Sita had been close for years, so that was the only reason I fucked with her. Yet and still, I didn't trust bitches. Chloe had taught me that lesson the hard way. Cherrie was real pretty and had major confidence. That bitch was ratchet as fuck though. With dark, smooth milk chocolate skin, almond shaped eyes and high cheek bones, she was stunning. At 5'3, she was thick, and probably weighted about one fifty.

Rucker's parking lot was flooded, and I was ready to see what was popping. We'd already had those Coronas and a blunt, so I was buzzing. Now I wanted some liquor. It took a minute for us to get in, but once we were inside, we managed to find an empty table.

Niggas and skimpy dressed bitches were wall to wall. Everybody was grubbing, drinking, dancing and some were playing pool. There were a lot of pool tables. After a while of sitting and waiting for a server to come over, we both were growing impatient.

There was a funny look on Cherrie's face as she looked at something behind me. "Oh shit..."

"What's wrong Cherrie?"

She was still staring off at something behind me.

"What the fuck you lookin' at?" Then I turned around.

"Xavia..."

There that nigga Duke was hugged up with some tall, light skinned bitch. That hoe had to be at least 5'8 and weighted no more than a buck twenty. The bitch was skinny as a rail with blonde weave down to her flat ass.

"Oh, but that nigga's s'posed to be out of fuckin' town." Jumping to my feet, I felt a surge of adrenaline course through my veins.

Cherrie got up to follow me. When I stood in front of Duke, he did a double take. That bitch had her back turned to me, so she didn't see us walk up.

"Thought yo' ass was out of town!" I yelled over the music and chatter.

That nigga didn't even respond to me. Instead, he grabbed old girl's hand and tried to walk off like I was going to just let that shit go. By that time, she'd looked back and was asking Duke who the fuck I was.

"Yeah, tell her who I am Duke. Let her know that we been fuckin' for six months. Tell her that we fucked in the bed you fuck her in too!" My hands were all in his face.

Duke had the audacity to push my hand away, while giving me a cold stare. It was like he hadn't just been sucking and licking on my pussy a few days before. It was like he hadn't sent me a bunch of bullshit ass presents for Valentine's day. It was like he hadn't fed me a bunch of bullshit lies along with money to keep me complacent and out of his business.

"You fuckin' her Duke?" The bitch asked like I hadn't just confirmed it already. "I should slap the fuckin' shit outta you!"

"Tiff, you already know how I do. I got money and I fuck other bitches. You my wife, ma. That's nothing." He had the nerve to cup her chin in his hand and flashed her that same loving look I'd seen.

"Yo' wife? For real Duke? You're fuckin' married!"

That shit infuriated me, because I didn't even care if he had a wife. What made me mad was the fact that he lied about that shit and was trying to play me in front of that ugly hoe. I was so damn angry, I jumped on that nigga and started punching him all in the face. When I looked, Cherrie was fighting that nigga's bitch. Security cleared us out of there. When we were outside Cherrie told me that bitch tried to pull my hair, so she stumped her ass out.

"Not that I expected that nigga to be all about me, but he ain't have to go out of his way to lie. Then he gon' make me look like I ain't shit 'round that bitch. Fuck that nigga and his wife."

The more niggas fucked me over, the more I lost my ability to feel anything.

"You tryna go somewhere else?" Cherrie glanced at me with a sympathetic look on her face.

There was no way I was going to let that nigga spoil my night, so we ended up going to a bar/lounge. After plenty of drinks, Cherrie was drunk as hell, so I had to drive. Man, I was drunk too, but that bitch was staggering and all. Once we were back at my apartment, I suggested that she spend the night instead of trying to drive back home.

She agreed and plopped on the sofa as soon as we walked in the door.

"You know you can sleep in Sita's bed. I'm sure she won't be back anytime soon," I suggested as I kicked my shoes off and proceeded to peel off my jeans.

"I'm good right here. I can't even make it to her room. As soon as I sober up, I'm gone."

"A'ight, goodnight girl. If you leave before I get up just lock the door behind you."

She mumbled something behind me that sounded like, okay goodnight. Stumbling into my room, I finished undressing and laid on top of the covers. I'd even taken off my underwear, because that liquor was making me feel extra hot.

As I lie there, I thought about how Duke had a whole damn wife. Not that it would've kept me from fucking with him, but why didn't he just tell me? The fact that six months went by and he hadn't mentioned that he was married made it easy for me to pull away. Then that nigga tried to downplay the shit like I was nothing but something for him to do to pass time. Oh, hell nah. I may not have been interested in being his wife, but I was far from being nothing to any man.

While my thoughts soared, I eventually drifted off into a restless sleep. A warm, tingling sensation between my thighs got my attention. Damn, was I having a wet dream? Ohhh... my clit was being gently and lovingly sucked and that shit felt so real. Damn, I was about to cum and as I reached down to touch the head of my lover, I felt a head full of hair. That's when my eyes snapped open and I saw Cherrie between my legs lapping up my pussy juices like a hungry pussycat. I wasn't fucking dreaming.

"Bitch! What the fuck you doin'?" By instinct, I kicked her in the face hard as fuck. As if in slow motion, she flew up off the bed and landed on the floor on her ass.

"The fuck Xa!" That bitch held on to her cheek and looked up at me with fear in her eyes.

I was already on my feet standing over her, ready to beat the life out of her ass. What made that bitch think it was okay to come in my room and start eating my pussy? Nah, I had to be dreaming. That shit couldn't be real.

"The hell you mean, bitch? You must've been doin' more than drinkin' and smokin' trees tonight! What the fuck?"

Balling up my fist, I grabbed her weave and was about to bash her face in when she begged for me not to.

"Don't! Don't Xa! I'm sorry. Fuck! I been wantin' you since the day we met." Tears fell from her eyes.

Damn, I had no idea the bitch was even bisexual.

"I ain't into women Cherrie and even if I was, why wouldn't you let me in on that shit!"

"Fuck, Sita gets down, so I thought you would too."

Wow. So Sita's freaky ass was fucking with bitches too? Why didn't that surprise me although she'd never mentioned that shit to me.

"Well, bitch, I ain't Sita. Just 'cause she lets you eat her pussy don't mean I'll let you eat mine. You know what, get the fuck out! Now! Don't ever come 'round me again. If you do, I'm kickin' yo' ass on sight."

"Damn Xa." She stood up and shook her head at me. "You know that shit felt good."

"Bitch, fuck you! If you don't get the fuck outta here, I'm gon' drag yo' ass out after I kill yo' disrespectful ass!"

Yeah, I was enjoying that shit, but that was before I knew she was the one eating me. At first, I thought I was dreaming. That bitch had to go. If she was eating Sita's pussy, she needed to stick with that, because I wasn't the one. Nasty ass hoe.

Sita walked toward the door and then turned to look at me. "Umm... don't tell Sita. I just thought after what happened wit' Duke, you'd finally be done wit' niggas. When I did that shit to Sita, she was cool wit' it. Shit, me and that bitch be on it. You just don't know that I'll change yo' whole fuckin' life."

Was that heifer still trying to convince me that eating my pussy was cool? It took everything in me not to grab my switchblade and gut that bitch.

"I ain't gon' tell you again Cherrie! I'm just gon' show you how much I don't like bitches!"

After I said that, she got the hint and left. I sat down on the bed not believing that shit had actually happened. With the quickness, I got up to take a shower. I had to wash that bitch's spit off my damn pussy. What made that shit even worse was the fact that she was right. That shit felt good as fuck. Still, I wasn't into bitches though.

* * *

About a month had passed by and any feelings I thought I had for Duke were long gone. I returned to living by Sita's philosophy. Somehow, I'd convinced myself not to feel anything for a man, and eventually I didn't. Cam was my go to nigga when shit went left with Duke.

He wanted to take me out to dinner and I kept right on bitching about needing a new outfit.

"But baby, I need something to wear. I can't go out in the same old shit."

"Man, you trip me out. All them clothes you got in yo' closet. It's cool though. I'll get you something to wear baby."

"A'ight let's go." I jumped up, leading him to the door.

We had been in the mall for less than fifteen minutes when I spotted Rahz and his crew. My mind kept repeating, fuck, oh shit, fuck, oh shit.

"I'on even feel like dealin' with this crowded ass mall. We can leave Cam. Fuck it, I'll wear something I already got."

"What? When have you gave a shit that the mall's crowded. We here now and you gon' get something."

Walking ahead, I held on to his wrist and attempted to pull him into a store so Rahz wouldn't see me. That was useless being that Rahz seemed to have the hawk-eye when it came to me. We hadn't seen each other, or talked in months, but that didn't stop him.

"Yo', Xa!" Rahz called out all loud over the hustle and bustle of shoppers.

Pretending not to hear him, I didn't respond. Cam stopped walking though.

"C'mon." I pulled him.

"Xa!" Rahz called out again, getting closer to us.

"Cam, damn, I said c'mon."

"You don't hear that nigga callin' yo' name? What you tryna hide?"

"Ain't nobody call me."

Rahz was getting closer and Cam wouldn't move. "Let's see what that nigga wants."

Rolling my eyes in annoyance, I went ahead and told him the truth before Rahz spilled the beans.

"A'ight, fuck it. His name's Rahz and I used to... deal wit' him a while back. I cut him off 'cause he's crazy as hell. That's why I was tryna leave. I wanted to keep y'all from havin' a... confrontation. He punched a dude in the face just for lookin' at me once."

Cam's eyes drifted off. "What he look like?"

"Dreadlocks, red shirt. He's coming in this direction."

"Ohh... that nigga. I know him. Lame, hatin' ass mufucka. He Jamaican and shit."

"Yeah."

That nigga Rahz was finally less than a foot from us.

"Damn star, it's been a long ass time. Wha' gwaan?" Rahz's eyes were glued to me.

"Don't run up on me talkin' like we cool and shit. I been cut yo' psycho ass off."

Rahz looked over at Cam. "Don't mi know yuh?"

"And? What if you do?" Cam had a look on his face that told me they had some deep-rooted hate between them that had nothing to do with me.

"Yeah, mi do know yuh bloodclat mufucka. Yuh was talkin' shit not too long ago." A slick ass grin appeared on Rahz's face. "We in di public now, but mi will see yo' punk ass in di streets."

"I hope so, mufucka." Cam was still mean mugging Rahz and his niggas. The threat Rahz had made didn't seem to sway him at all.

"C'mon Cam, let's go."

My nerves were shot as he kept staring those niggas down. Slowly, but surely, he walked off and we left the mall. Once we were in the car, he drove off and just looked straight ahead without talking to me.

"Say something Cam."

"I ain't got shit to say. I'm just gon' take you home."

With a pout, I leaned back in my seat. "So, it's like that? We ain't goin' out now?"

"You got secrets and shit shawty. Why you playin' games?"

"Cam, I ain't playin' games. That shit wit' Rahz was nothin' to fuckin' talk about. I met him way before anything happened between us. That's like me bein' mad 'cause you got a baby mama. Don't act like I couldn't have fucked wit' a nigga before you."

He seemed to calm down and then his hand was on my thigh. With a squeeze, he leaned over to kiss me.

"You're right. It's just, me and that fuck nigga already got beef. Now shit just got real."

Not knowing what to think about that, I tried to downplay it. It wasn't like I was fucking Rahz. I was sure that eventually, he'd let it go and move on with his life. Cam didn't bother to explain what their beef was about about and I didn't ask.

Chapter 9

Miami

2014

Over the course of a month and a half that shit with Rahz only got worse. His jealousy had turned into an obsession. He would send me all types of gifts and even pop up at my apartment professing his undying love for me. Although I'd changed my number, somehow, he ended up calling me. That was one thing I could not figure out. Did he know somebody at Verizon?

I'd even resorted to calling the damn cops, but of course they couldn't do shit unless a bitch ended up dead somewhere. It got to the point where I realized I had to deal with Rahz on my own. Cam and my uncles were willing to protect me, but they couldn't always be around. Knowing that the police wasn't going to do shit made me even more vulnerable and paranoid.

It was early in the afternoon and I was home alone. Sita was spending time with some pro-football player who was in town. My phone rang and scared the shit out of me. It was Rahz and that was the third time I'd changed my number in a month's time. What the fuck? I decided right then to change carriers, because I had no clue how he kept getting my number.

"Look nigga, my man is on the way over and I'd appreciate it if you'd just leave me the fuck alone."

All he did was breath on the other line. Looking out of the window, I wondered if he was outside of my apartment. Instead of staying there to find out, I decided to go out for a little while. Rahz was trying his best to keep me from living my life, but I wasn't going to give him that power over me.

Miami was hot as fuck, but the weather would sometimes be mild. It was about eighty-two degrees on a clear day, so I decided to throw on some tights and go for a jog. There was a park with a nice jogging trail not far from Cam's house. We'd ran together there plenty of times before. I called to ask him to meet me there, but he didn't answer his phone. Regardless of that, I decided to go anyway.

After my mile-long jog was over, I felt refreshed, but thirsty as fuck. Downing my bottle of water, I looked over to my left and guess who I saw? Yes, Cam's baby mama Ebony. After I threw my empty water bottle away, I made my way over to that bitch.

Finally, Cam wasn't around to keep me from stumping a hole in her ass. The only thing was, their daughter was with her. Camille was on the swing and Ebony stood behind her pushing. The human side of me that wasn't so savage told me to just keep it moving. Then my savage side said, fuck that shit. If that bitch pops off at the mouth, punch her in it. I didn't give a fuck if her daughter was with her ass or not. That hoe tended to talk shit when she had Camille, so I was going to show her the consequences.

When Ebony spotted me, she rolled her eyes and then started doing what she did best.

"Oh, my fuckin' god. Are you stalkin' Cam or what bitch?"

"Nah bitch. You must be the one stalkin' him."

"You gon' call me a bitch around my baby? I told that nigga you a petty ass hoe wit' no class."

"Look who's talkin'." I smirked at her. "You the one who called me a bitch first. Then you called me a hoe in front in your daughter. If you don't give a fuck what you say 'round her, I don't either bitch."

She just kept right on pushing that swing and I stood there fucking with that bitch.

"Girl bye. I ain't thinkin' 'bout you," she hissed.

"Oh, okay. Now that Cam ain't here you ain't thinkin' bout me. It's mighty funny when that nigga's around you be ready to pop off and act like you wanna throw hands. Camille being around ain't never stopped you before. What's up wit' all that mouth now bitch? Ain't nobody around to stop you. You wanna beat my ass so bad, so why don't you try it."

That hoe waved me off like I hadn't just said some real ass shit. "My daughter is out here, so I ain't got time to entertain yo' ratchet ass."

"Oh really." I moved closer to her and put my finger in her face. "You don't wanna beat my ass now?"

"You better back the fuck up bitch!"

She looked afraid as hell as she stood there actually holding her baby's swing in front of her.

"You scared ain't you bitch?" With a malicious smile, I reached up and smacked her in the face hard as hell.

"You gon' hit me with my baby out here!" She screamed with her face turning beet red.

As I stood there waiting for her to buck, she turned around and picked her daughter up from the swing instead. Holding the toddler in her arms, she walked away from me and pulled out her cell phone.

"Who you callin' scared bitch? Put her down and fight me! The stroller's right there. Put her in it. She can't get out. Don't worry. She's already heard you talk shit to me, so she might as well watch you get fucked up out this bitch."

She put her phone up to her ear. "Do you know that bitch you fuckin' is tryna fight me while I got yo' daughter with me! I told you she ain't shit! I'm pressin' assault charges on this hoe!" With that said she hung up and then made another call.

With a smirk on my face, I knocked the phone out of her hand. "Don't be tellin' Cam on me like I'm some fuckin' child, bitch. I ain't Camille."

That's when I knocked her upside her head again. Man, I wanted her to put Camille down so bad. I wasn't trying to hurt her, but her mother had tried me too many times. There was no way I was going to let that bitch get away with that shit.

"You gon' keep hittin' me while I'm holdin' my daughter!" She screamed wishing I'd leave her alone because of Camille.

"She don't need you to hold her bitch! The only reason you holdin' her is 'cause you don't want me to chin check yo' ass! I ain't hit yo' daughter. I hit you bitch! You wanna fight me so bad and now when you got the opportunity you suddenly care that yo' daughter's around! Wow! You talk all that shit, but ain't gon' do shit."

That bitch walked off to her car with her daughter in her arms and left the damn stroller behind. A bitch like me still wasn't satisfied. Once I got my hands on her, I was going to drag her ass.

"Scary ass bitch!" I yelled after her as she drove off like a bat out of hell.

As I laughed, I headed to my own car and called Cam. He still wasn't answering, and I wondered what the fuck was going on with him. Once I left the park, I went to his crib and rang the doorbell, but he didn't answer. Against my will, I went home not able to shake the feeling that something just wasn't right.

* * *

It was after two am and Rahz had called me at least twenty times. Sita was still gone, Cam wasn't answering his phone and my uncles weren't either. So, I called the police department.

"Ma'am, we can't arrest somebody for calling you too much," the officer told me in an impatient tone.

"I'm tellin' you he's stalkin' me and…"

"You will have to take him to court and try to get a protective order against him. If he violates that, then you can have him arrested, but until then…"

Before he could even finish, I hung up the phone. The law was not on my side, so I was on my own.

Rahz sent me a text since I wasn't answering his calls.

When ur nigga gets here I got a surprise waitin for him.

That made me call him. Where the fuck was he? Was he watching me.

"Yo' ass is even more psycho than I thought. I called the police and they on the way. I don't want you and I wish you'd just get that through your head."

"I'm right in front of yo' building."

"Just leave Rahz, please."

"See, that's how y'all Yankee bitches do a mufucka who go outta his way to make yuh happy. Just 'cause yuh fine and some other nigga show yuh some attention, yuh just drop me? Nah, it don't work like dat! What makes him a better mon than mi? Huh? Tell me dat!"

"He don't act crazy like you! That makes him better. You never made me happy nigga. Bye

Rahz. You better leave before the cops come." I hung up on him and peeked through the blinds in the living room. That crazy asshole was parked in Sita's space. He turned his headlights on and blinked them twice. Shaking my head, I never thought he'd go any further than that.

Fifteen minutes later when I looked, his car was gone. Not able to relax, I couldn't go to sleep. Nothing was on TV, so I turned it off and decided to go up to my room. I heard a loud bang that made me even more nervous. Maybe Sita was back. Then I heard footsteps coming down the hall.

It had to be Sita, or Aunt B, since she was the only other person who had a key. One thing I did was make sure the door was locked. Peeking through my bedroom's blinds, I saw that neither Sita or Aunt B's car was outside. My blood ran cold and I rushed to lock my bedroom door. Before I could it opened and hit me in the face. The impact took my breath away and I looked up to see Rahz walking towards me.

"How the fuck did you get in here?" Stepping back, I wished I had a damn gun. Making a mental note to get one if I made it out of that situation alive, I tried to play it cool.

"Mi got mi ways. When mi wan' somethin', mi get it. Where ya so called mon at? Huh?"

"Just leave, and I won't call the cops..."

He laughed and walked closer to me. "Mi thought yuh already called dem."

At a loss for words, I didn't know what to say.

"What yuh call dem for anyway? Mi ain't done shit to yuh. Mi just wanna talk. Mi didn't mean to hit yuh wit' the door. Yuh walked into it."

That nigga had the nerve to be smiling at me like I wanted him in my bedroom.

"What do you want to talk about Rahz?" Tears burned my eyes and caressed my cheeks like hot embers.

"Don't cry baby."

"You're scarin' me."

"Mi not tryna scare yuh. Mi just want what we had. Mi was feelin' yuh and you fucked me over. Was mi not good to yuh?"

"Rahz, it wasn't what you thought it was between us. I tried, but it didn't work out. I'm sorry."

Quickening his pace, he was right in front of me, so close that I could smell his rancid breath. Eventually I had nowhere to run, because my bed was right behind me. He touched my cheek before running his fingers through my hair. A shiver traveled up and down my spinal cord.

"Mi love yuh and mi miss dat wet, tight, fat pum pum." When he tried to kiss me, I turned away.

"You don't love me. You think you do, but you don't."

Staring at me, he then grabbed my arm and twisted it behind my back. "Since yuh don't wanna give mi di pussy, mi guess mi will take it."

"No, Rahz, please." His hand was over my mouth muffling my screams as he pushed me back on the bed and climbed on top of me.

All the yelling and kicking I did only seemed to fuel his fire. In no time, he had his dick out. Standing over me, he dragged it against my lips and tried to force it in my mouth. When I wouldn't suck it, he slapped me in the face.

"Open your mouth yuh, bloodclot bitch!"

With tears cascading down my stinging cheek, I opened my mouth and he pushed his dick down my throat causing me to gag.

"Now suck dat shit like yuh mean it, or mi gon' kill yuh!"

Slobbering on that nigga's dick, I deep throated that shit with thoughts of biting it off. Without seeing a gun, I knew he had one on him and even if he didn't, he could kill me with his bare hands.

As he came in my mouth, I made sure I swallowed that shit down. Almost choking, I wanted to spit that bitter tasting shit out so bad.

"Swallow bitch! Mi don't know why yuh trippin'. It ain't like yuh ain't tasted dis dick before."

As he slid down between my legs, I stared up at him trying to look pitiful. "No Rahz, don't, please."

He'd just busted a nut, but his dick was rock hard as he ripped my panties off. Grabbing my thighs, he spread them open roughly and entered me even harder.

"OWWW!"

He slapped me in the face. "Shut the fuck up and take dis dick!"

That nigga was fucking me so hard, it felt like he was stabbing me in my guts. He thrusted inside of my depths with such anger and vigor, it was as if he was tearing me apart.

"Rahz... shit... please stop!"

His hand was over my mouth and he kept slapping me with his other hand.

"Didn't mi say shut di fuck up! Mi gon' shut yuh up, rassclat!"

As I closed my eyes, I couldn't stop whimpering. The pain was unbearable, and I just wished he'd cum already. Something told me that he wouldn't since he'd busted a nut already.

"Damn right, bitch! Dis pussy belongs to me! Mi gon' take that shit whenever mi want to!" A huge glob of his spit landed on my face.

What felt like an eternity passed as he grinded frantically inside of me. My pussy was dry and raw at that point. I could feel the lips swelling and my walls tearing with each of his deep thrusts. At that point, I'd passed out a few times from the excruciating pain. As I tried my best to run from his dick's assault, he just held me in place.

Finally, his face contorted and his eyes rolled back. "Arrrggghhh... fuuuuccckkk!"

He grabbed me by my hair and pulled. I just prayed that he'd hurry up. He was not a small man and was packing at least eight and a half inches of thick dick. That shit was like a damn toddler's leg. I'd had sex with him willingly in the past, but that shit was different.

"Ohhh... shit..." His dick jerked inside of me and then he collapsed on my chest.

His sweat made his skin stick to me and I was so damn disgusted. All I wanted was for him to get off me and leave. Either that, or I was going to find something to end his sorry ass life with.

As he stood up and fixed his clothes, my hate for him festered like an infection. I just balled up in the fetal position and sobbed uncontrollably. That mufucka didn't give zero fucks.

"Dat shit was good as hell baby." He kissed my cheek and I flinched.

Then I watched him leave the room. The sound of the front door slamming was the only thing that made me get up. The doorknob was intact, so I knew he'd picked the lock. He'd told me there was no lock he couldn't pick. Why hadn't I seen that as a red flag?

Instead of calling the sorry ass police, I just locked the door back and added the chain. That was my damn mistake the first time. Running to the bathroom, I turned the shower on and got in. It didn't matter how much I scrubbed, I didn't feel clean. As much as I wanted to report the rape, I couldn't. We'd had sex in the past and they'd probably think it was consensual. Although I'd called them at first, that was to prevent what had already happened. What the fuck would they do at that point other than judge me?

After two hours or more in the tub, my skin was bright red and wrinkled. Climbing between the covers, I cried myself to sleep after changing my sheets and comforter. Actually, I threw that shit in the trash. My excuse for the bruises on my face was that I'd been mugged. I never told anybody the truth about that shit, until I had no choice.

* * *

The two pink lines that stared back at me only made my problems worse. Almost three months had passed since the night Rahz had raped me. Sita was waiting in my room for the verdict. It had to be Rahz's baby, because I was only fucking Cam and we always used condoms.

Rahz hadn't bothered me since and it was probably because he was afraid that I'd called the cops. Although, I hadn't, I wished I had. There was not a day that went by that I didn't fear what he'd do to me next. I hadn't even said shit to Cam.

"You knocked up ain't it bitch?" Sita said when she saw the fresh tears in my eyes

"Uh huh."

"You crazy. Don't you know that you don't let these sorry, nasty dick niggas hit raw?" Her eyes were wide and full of disgust.

Fresh tears welled up in my eyes. "Sita, I do use condoms. This is... different. I'm pregnant by... Rahz."

"Oh my god! What the fuck is wrong wit' you? You let that mufucka nut in you? Why the hell would you even fuck him again?"

That was when I blew up. "Why don't you shut the fuck up and listen for once! Damn! He raped me, okay. He broke into our apartment when you were out and forced himself on me. I told him no, but he didn't give a fuck! He kept slappin' me and tellin' me to shut the fuck up. I was scared that he was goin' to kill me. I know he carries a gun at all times. You know I wouldn't have fucked that nigga by choice. I know how crazy he is!" My sobs were out of control as I fell to my knees.

Sita looked stunned as she got down on her knees in front of me. "I'm sorry Xa. Why didn't you say something? You should've reported him for that shit."

"I know..." Wiping my eyes, I let her help me up to my feet.

"Have you seen him since?"

"No, I haven't seen him, and I don't want to. He picked the lock, so it didn't look like he broke in. Plus, I got a history of fuckin' him. They won't believe me."

"You don't know that."

"It don't matter now. I'm fuckin' pregnant by that nigga."

Sita wiped my tears away. "What you gon' do?"

"I'm gon' have it."

"You gon' tell Cam it's his?"

"No, I'm gon' tell him the truth. Regardless of what you think about men, Cam's a good person. I can't lie to him like that. As far as an abortion is concerned, no matter how this baby was conceived, that's not an option. I can't, and I won't do that. This baby is still part of me."

Besides, I wanted someone that I could love on my own terms who would love me back unconditionally. Maybe that baby would be the turning point in my life. Maybe, just maybe my shattered heart would become whole again.

Chapter 10

Miami

2014

More than two weeks passed before I told Cam. That was only because he'd fired up a blunt and tried to pass it to me. When I refused, he knew something was up. It was time to confess.

"You refusin' the blunt?" Cam looked shocked as he blew smoke out of his nose.

"Yeah..."

"Uh... why?"

In a low voice, I said, "I'm pregnant."

That nigga choked and then started coughing. "What? You what?"

"Not by you Cam. I'm pregnant by Rahz."

His angry eyes met mine and I could see the hurt in them. He took another pull from the blunt without saying a word.

I continued. "About three months ago he broke into my apartment and raped me. I wasn't mugged. He'd been stalkin' me for months and I even tried to call you, but you wouldn't answer your phone. That was the same day I got into that shit wit' Ebony."

He'd explained to me later that Camilla had hid his phone under the sofa cushion and he couldn't find it because it was on silent.

Cam wouldn't even look at me.

"I would've never fucked him willingly. You gotta believe me."

Standing up, he left the room. He came back with a Corona and sat back down on the sofa.

"I believe you. I'm just mad as hell. What you plannin' to do?"

"Have it."

With a nod, he took a long sip of his beer. "Why you ain't tell me before now, so that nigga would be taken care of?"

"I'on know. I guess I was afraid you wouldn't believe me. That's the same reason I didn't call the cops."

"You sure you wanna have it?"

"Yes."

"That nigga deserves to get his wig split. I'm gon' handle his ass."

"Fuck Rahz. He's outta my life. I guess he did what he wanted and now he's done. I think he's gonna leave me alone for good."

"What if he finds out 'bout the baby and wants to be back in yo' life? What then?"

"Me and Sita are movin' next month since our lease is about to be up. We gon' need three bedrooms anyway. There's no way he's comin' near my baby. I guess I'll deal wit' that shit if I have to."

Cam sighed and shook his head. "I'm gon' kill that nigga, point blank period. You still workin'?"

"Yeah, but when I start showin', I know they gon' want me to take off."

"It's gon' work out. It's not my baby, but I got you shawty. Straight up. I just wanna kill that nigga so fuckin' bad for violatin' you like that."

"What's y'all beef anyway? You never told me."

"I didn't plan to."

"Why?"

"Cause that shit don't concern you."

"Well, it does now Cam."

With a sigh, he put his beer down on a coaster on the coffee table.

"Not too long ago I met this nigga mufuckas call Jafari. He was braggin' 'bout how he had a connect to some pure, uncut Columbian blow. I don't trust niggas I don't know, so I checked out his credentials. Turned out, he rolled with Rahz. I'd done business wit' Rahz before over the years and shit. For some dumb ass reason, I did trust him. The whole time they were plottin' on a nigga. They wanted my clientele and my money without givin' me the product. When it was time to the do the exchange, his connect started bustin' and shit. Next thing I know, it's a shoot-out. Two of my front men got killed. Them mufucka's fucked me over and got away with my money. Me and my niggas retaliated, and we got Jafari. That nigga Rahz ran to Jamaica and I just saw him again when we was at the mall that day. Time had made that shit cool off, but it's heated up again."

"Damn, this shit's crazy Cam. I don't want you gettin' in no shit because of me."

"He raped you. This shit done got real fuckin' personal. Don't you worry. I got you and the baby."

Walking over to me, he put his hand under my chin. "Keep your head up Queen. Don't let nah nigga take yo' pride yo'. Never give a mufucka that power over you." Leaning over, he kissed my lips softly.

That one act of affection along with his words made me feel like somebody in the world gave a fuck about me. "Cam, you ain't gotta do that."

Putting his index finger to my lips, he shushed me. "I care about you, so just let me do it. Okay?

"Okay. Just promise me you won't go after Rahz. I couldn't take anything happenin' to you."

"I can't make that promise shawty. One thing I've never done is lie to you."

Resting my head on his chest, I was grateful to have him in my corner. He rubbed my back soothingly.

"It's gon' be okay shawty. I promise. I got you and I got lil' man, lil' mama, or whatever it is."

We both managed to laugh despite the situation.

As much as I wanted to trust Cam, I didn't know if he'd really be there no matter what. I'd been through so much with the opposite sex, but I believed him.

* * *

Four months later

Damn, I was big as hell at seven months pregnant. My fat ass was wobbling and all as I tried to get to the kitchen. I knew that Cam was on his way over, but he had a key. Since we'd moved into our new place, Sita was hardly home, so she didn't care if he had a key. Besides, I was big and pregnant, so it was necessary.

When I heard the front door open and close, I didn't panic. It was just Cam. I had a doctor's appointment at eleven and it was a little after eight in the morning. My greedy ass was trying to find something to eat before we left. He walked up and wrapped his arms around my extended waist.

"Good morning baby," he said as he kissed my neck.

"Good morning babe. I'm hungry."

"What's new," he laughed.

Slapping him playfully, I said, "I'm pregnant. What's your excuse?"

"I'm just greedy." He grinned and then kissed my lips softly. "C'mon, I'll feed you before we get to the doctor's office. Okay fatty?"

"Okay," I giggled and grabbed my purse before slipping my swollen feet into some flip flops.

We went to Ihop and I wolfed down a Belgium waffle with maple syrup, bacon, sausage, grits, cheese eggs and a side of pancakes. That shit was so good.

"Damn, slow down shawty. You gon' have my lil' girl fat as hell too."

"Shut up Cam." I laughed and sipped my orange juice.

My appointment went well, and my baby girl was doing good. Cam was the best thing that had ever happened to me and I was glad that I hadn't shut him out completely. That nigga paid all my bills, including my medical expenses and he wasn't even the father of my child. Something told me that he wished he was though.

He'd told me time and time again that he didn't want me to have to depend on the system. "That's how black families fail. Dependin' on a government that don't give a shit 'bout us. They want our women to need them. It's like this. The black woman can't get any benefits with a man in the home, so they hold all that shit over your heads to get rid of the black man. Now there ain't no daddies around. That's the plan. It's a crutch that they want you to depend on forever to keep you crippled. That's why I'll hustle 'till the day I die. Fuck them mufuckas in DC. They can all kiss my black ass," he'd told me.

"Damn, lil' mama's bein' feisty today." Rubbing my stomach, I tried to get comfortable in my seat.

Cam reached over and felt my belly with his free hand as he steered with the other. "Oh yeah, she takes after her mama."

The light turned green and Cam removed his hand from my stomach to drive.

"Umm, does it bother you that she ain't yours?"

"To be honest, it did a little at first. Fuck that though. She needs a daddy and being the one who made her don't make me that. I'm the one doin' that daddy shit and that's all that matters. That's my shawty."

"Why you doin' this for me Cam? Your kindness scares me, because from what I know, that shit does not last."

Cam looked over at me. "You need to know that all men ain't the same. You been through a lot of shit. I know you ain't told me everything, but I can see the pain in your eyes sometimes. That's even when you claim you happy. It's hard enough to survive in these streets when you got somebody, so it's worse on your own. I live that life every day. You don't need to, and your baby girl don't either. I wanna make it easier and on top of that, I love you shawty. That's why."

His words had taken me aback and I was stunned. Rubbing my belly, I thought about what he'd just said.

"You so hard," he said before turning the radio up.

Turning it down, I told him, "You gotta try to understand Cam. I ain't never told you about what made me come here, so I guess you can't. It's a real good reason why you see pain in my eyes, even when I'm supposed to be happy. I have a way of holdin' shit in. That ain't good, especially not when I'm pregnant."

So, I spilled my guts about my past with my mother, Eddie and Chloe. When I finished, I wiped my flowing tears away. Cam pulled up to a gas station.

"Damn, I'm sorry that shit happened to you shawt. I ain't know. I'd never do no shit like that to you. I can tell you that 'till I'm blue in the face, but action speaks louder than words. I'll show you." Pulling me into a hug, he gave me a loving kiss before going in the store.

Cam got back in the car with a box of Black and Milds. He put them in his pocket and drove off.

"You a'ight?"

"Yeah, I'm good, for once."

All I wanted to do was get back in bed and cuddle with him. I yawned, stretched, leaned back and closed my eyes.

"You sleepy?"

"Hell yeah. I wanna get in my bed and go to sleep. Well, after I eat... again."

"I'll feed you, but after that can I lay down with you?"

"Yeah, I was hopin' you would."

My pregnant ass was horny as shit. We'd only fucked a few times since I found out I was pregnant. At first, Cam seemed to feel some type of way about me being knocked up by Rahz. He came around though.

When we finally made it to my crib, I didn't even make it to my bed. The plush sofa looked good and was exactly where my ass landed. Cam positioned himself behind me and held me close to him. Food was the furthest thing from my mind as I drifted off to sleep.

When my eyes fluttered open and focused, I saw Rahz standing over me. Before I could scream, he stuck something in my mouth. The way I was moving and flailing my arms must've woke Cam up. He was also a light sleeper and I was grateful. Quickly, he drew his fist back and tried to punch Rahz, since he didn't have his gun on him. He'd already removed it from his waist and put it on the end table. It wasn't there anymore, so I knew that Rahz had it.

That's when I heard a gun cock. Cam drew his fist back.

"Fuck, you ain't gotta do this shit man," he said calmly. "Let her go. This shit's between us."

"Fuck yuh. Mi here to talk to di mother of my child."

I couldn't help but hate the accent that I once loved. All I could do was cry and think about my baby. My sobs got louder and that seemed to make Rahz even angrier.

"Shut di fuck up!" He shot towards the ceiling and I jumped thinking he'd shot me.

Rahz spoke directly in my ear. "Mi know yuh didn't tink mi would just leave yuh alone for dat mufucka to raise my fuckin' yute. Mi know di pickney's mine. Mi meant to nut in yuh."

Cam's face was contorted in anger. I knew he wished he'd kept his gun on him. The only reason he put it on the end table was out of fear of it going off. He'd done that to ensure me and my baby's safety, but it was ironic that he needed that gun to save us.

"Mi loved yuh! Yuh fucked mi, so mi fucked yuh! Mi had to make sure yuh tied to mi forever. Then yuh still fuck that lame ass nigga! Mi should kill' yuh both!"

Then I heard Cam's voice. "The baby ain't yours. She's mine."

"Nigga please. Mi know dat's my baby. I don't miss. Now shut di fuck up!" Rahz pointed the gun in Cam's face.

Suddenly he pointed the gun back at me. "Like mi was sayin', now yuh fuckin' him wit' mi seed inside of yuh? Yuh fuckin' slut! Mi must admit, it's something 'bout yuh that make mi do crazy shit! Mi wanted yuh to have mi seed, but now mi want yuh dead! Mi would rather see yuh and my pickney dead than see yuh wit' this mufucka! Mi wan' dat pussy one more time though, right in front of dat nigga."

Cam looked down at me helplessly. He wanted to do something, but he knew that Rahz would make good on his threats.

"Kill me nigga. Fuck that. You really wanna kill me, so do that shit. Let Xa and the baby live."

At that moment I realized that you couldn't make a fair deal with the devil. Rahz's wicked laughter was loud and evil.

"Nigga, mi was gon' kill ya' black ass anyway!"

"Kill me, but leave her alone. She been through enough already."

"Mi can fuck my baby mama if mi wan' too nigga, don't yuh fuck yours?" Rahz smirked at him and I was in turmoil.

Closing my eyes, I said a prayer for me, my child and Cam. Then I felt a commotion that made my eyes fly open. Cam was trying to wrestle the gun out of Rahz's hand. Then he pushed me out of harm's way. I landed on the floor with a thud just as I watched Rahz get control of the gun. That shit was pointed right in Cam's face.

POW!

I heard the explosion and then saw Cam's face splatter across the room in bloody pieces. My screams were hysterical as I cried out for the one man who seemed to give a fuck about me. It was my fault that he was dead. He'd sacrificed his life for me and my unborn child. However, that didn't seem to make Rahz take any mercy out on me.

There was a demonic scowl on his face as he towered over me. Holding my hands over my face, I tried to shield myself from the assault of his closed fists. He pummeled my face and body with punches before he stripped me naked and took advantage of my ravished body. After he'd fuck me, he'd beat me. Then he started kicking and stumping my stomach. I held on to my belly trying to protect my baby. Eventually I'd had enough, and my body shut down.

* * *

Almost a month later, I woke up in the ICU from a coma. My aunt and cousin were both by my side. The doctors and nurses rushed in to check my vitals and make sure that I was okay. All I wanted to know was if my baby survived. I knew that Cam was gone and that was enough to make me want to die. Why didn't I tell him that I loved him back, because I did? Damn, I regretted that shit. The only thing that gave me any hope was the life that I carried in my womb.

When I reached down to feel my belly, it felt flatter. There was no way I was still pregnant. My stomach was huge before that shit with Rahz. Did I have my baby early? Was she okay? Was there any way I could've changed fate? If only I'd looked back when Cam and I were at that gas station. I would've seen that nigga following us.

"My baby..." I whispered hoarsely.

After what seemed like an eternity, a nurse finally told me that she'd died. My baby was gone.

"NOOOOOOOOO!!!!!!!!!" My aunt and cousin had to restrain me to keep me from pulling my IV and all the other tubes out. I was devastated and there was nothing that could ease the hurt. It didn't matter how much pain medication they fed me. They'd put something in my IV to calm me down and in no time, I was still.

No matter how my body felt, my mind was going a mile a minute. I even heard my aunt telling Sita that she hoped the cops caught Rahz. Personally, I wanted street justice. Prison was too good for his ass. He'd taken everything that I gave a shit about away from me. Yeah, Eddie had broken my heart into a million pieces, but Rahz had snatched my soul.

Chapter 11

Atlanta

2017

Alicia had mixed some drinks and cooked some hot wings and fries later the next night. I'd spent most of the day with my mom. We went to the movies to see *Girls Trip*, had lunch and went shopping. Now it was bonding time with my bestie. I'd just filled her in on what had gone down with Rahz and Cam. She was very sympathetic as I cried familiar tears. Some of those tears were out of guilt. There was no way I couldn't blame myself for Cam and my baby's death.

"You gotta forgive yourself Xa. Believe it, or not, it wasn't your fault. You had no control over that maniac." She wiped her eyes because she'd been crying too. "You're still here to start over. Not that I feel your life is more valuable than Cam's or your baby, but God spared your life for a reason." Reaching out, she held my hand. "You've been through hell and back. I know this, but believe me, you have people in your life that love you. You're gettin' your relationship right with your mom and you need that. No matter what, I'm always here for you. I love you girl, so no more disappearing shit."

We shared a hug. "I really needed this Licia," I whispered through the tears. "Everything the past five years has been so negative. I mean, some things are good, but... I'on even know if it's worth the drama anymore."

Alicia looked like she was in deep thought.

"You listenin' to me?" I slapped her on the thigh lightly as I asked.

"Yeah, I was just thinkin' 'bout something. Anyway, speakin' of the past, you need to patch things up with Chloe."

"Man, fuck Chloe. Here we got wit' that shit again. Why I gotta be the one to patch shit up wit' her? She fucked my man and I'll never forgive her. She was my friend before I even met you. We were in kindergarten together. You moved beside me when I was seven. She knew how deeply I loved Eddie. She didn't give a fuck about me then, so she shouldn't give a fuck about me now. Don't bring that hoe's name up again."

Alicia shook her head at me and went back to eating.

"What?"

"What you mean what? That was years ago. We are older now and Chloe regrets that shit. Why can't you just talk to her and get some closure. Y'all ain't gotta be friends no more, but this anger you're carrying around isn't good for you. I love you both and I would love for us to be close like we used to be." Tears were on her cheeks again and she wiped them away with a paper towel.

"She killed all that. Like I told you before, it doesn't matter how many years have gone by. I can't forgive her, and I won't. She can be your friend Licia. That's between y'all. I'd never make you choose between us. You just keep the grimy bitch out of my face and we good. That's all I gotta say. Can we change the subject? Please." My voice was filled with anger.

"Damn, she must really make your blood boil." Alicia looked shocked. "I feel sorry for her if you see her. All that pent-up anger gon' make you do something you'll regret."

"If I do see the bitch, I might let go of all that pent-up anger on her. I doubt if I'll regret it, so, I feel sorry for that bitch too. Now, like I said, can we please change the subject."

"Okay, shit, I'on remember ever seein' you this mad about anything since I've know you."

"Well, you never had a reason to before your brother fucked my friend and changed the course of my life. We were supposed to get married, have babies and be happy. No, instead, I moved to Miami and a once, innocent, sweet girl is all fucked up! That's Eddie and that bitch's fault! Don't blame me for bein' angry! I have every fuckin' right to be!"

"Okay, okay, you're right, but I'm just sayin..."

"Let it go," I said calmly. "I don't need a therapist right now Licia."

"A'ight... shit...

Maybe Eddie and I were just too attached back then. I for one was very clingy, because I never wanted to lose him. We spent way too much time together and we were so young at that. It was as if I always had to be right under him. Maybe that scared him and made him unfaithful to me. I was sure he loved me, but what if he felt held down by the weight of my love?

Alicia stood up and cleared the table of our empty plates. Jermaine and the girls were due back any minute. They'd gone out for pizza and a movie. Just as Alicia and I left the kitchen and sat down on the sofa, the door opened. Jermaine walked in carrying both girls. They were knocked out.

"Hey baby." He kissed Alicia and then glanced at me. "What's up Xa?"

"Nothing. Drunk as hell."

He chuckled as he walked off to go lay the girls down. Then he came back and sat down in the recliner.

"Well, I guess I'll get goin'." I stood up.

Jermaine gave me a look like I was crazy. "Ain't no need for you to drive home drunk. You a guest here. I mean, we only got two bedrooms, but you can crash on the sofa."

He got up and came back with linens and a comforter. Alicia stood up as he made the sofa up all nice and comfy for me. We all ended up drinking and laughing until the wee hours of the morning. Neither of them brought Eddie, or Chloe up. That was a good thing and I slept like a baby on that sofa.

* * *

The next morning, I woke up with a banging ass headache and a full bladder. Running to the bathroom, I looked up at the wall clock on the way. It was nine thirty-five. Even their kids slept late, because it was quiet as hell. After I peed, I laid back down on the sofa. My plan was to leave in a little while, but my head was killing me. When I heard a knock on the door, I groaned.

Dragging myself up, I went to see who it was since nobody else was going to. Besides, they just kept knocking and then decided to ring the doorbell. Damn. The sight of him made my head hurt even more. Opening the door, I told him, "Everybody's sleep."

A sly smile was on Eddie's face. "I ain't know you was here. I told my mom you in town and she mad you ain't came to see her yet."

"Well, I'm leavin' tomorrow. Licia tried to link us up, but your mom had to work. Tell her I'm sorry I missed her. Uh, if you comin' in, I'm leavin'. You know what, I need to leave anyway. You come on in."

Stepping aside, I watched his muscular frame move past me. Damn, he smelled so good. As I closed the door, he walked over the sofa and sat down. I sat across from him and put on my shoes.

"You still look good as hell when you wake up."

Sighing in frustration, the compliment didn't faze me. "Don't talk to me Eddie. I got a headache."

I folded the linens and blanket and placed them neatly on the sofa.

"Oh, Tell Licia and Maine I said thanks for the hospitality."

With that said, I left without uttering another word. When I got to my car, I realized that I'd left my car keys on the coffee table. Reluctantly, I walked back up the steps. Before I could even knock on the door, Eddie opened it with my keys in his hand. I tried to grab them, but he held them up out of my reach.

"You can't leave without these," he teased, smirking at me.

"You play too much? Why you still act like a lil' ass boy? It's cause you a punk ass mama's boy. You still ain't grew the fuck up. Gimme my fuckin' keys, so I can go!"

That nigga still seemed to know how to get under my skin. Stepping out on the porch, his smirk turned into a sexy, alluring smile.

"You know I still want you. You the only woman for me Xa. I'm convinced of that shit. You left your keys because you really don't wanna go. You know you want me too."

"Nope, I'm not that needy little girl anymore, so I don't want you." Reaching for my keys, I got even angrier when he held them up again.

"You can't go nowhere, so you gotta stay and talk to me."

"We ain't got shit to talk about Eddie. How many times do I have to tell you that? Why're you wasting your time? Stop actin' like a damn three year old and gimme my keys."

"It's no chance for us, ever?" His facial expression was more serious as he stared down into my eyes and handed me my keys.

"None." Without looking back, I walked off to my car.

"I still love you so much Xa."

"Uh huh, whatever. Bye Eddie."

Heading back to my mother's, I hoped she had some Tylenol or something. I'd looked for some pain pills in Alicia's medicine cabinet, but there were none. Ever since Rahz assaulted me, I had the worst headaches.

When I got to my mom's I went straight for her medicine cabinet in the bathroom in her bedroom. There were some Motrin and Aspirin. I took two of the Motrin, downed some water and laid down on her bed to go back to sleep. Hopefully I'd feel better when I woke up.

* * *

Miami
2015

Due to the injuries and swelling to my brain, the doctors had to put me in a medically induced coma. That was to minimize the damage to my brain. My legs hadn't been used in weeks, so I was suffering from slight atrophy. It was like my muscles were made of mush, so I had to go through physical therapy for a month. After that, I was released from the hospital.

Two months had gone by since the attack. It was a new year and Rahz was still on the loose. My fear was on one hundred, because I had no clue if he'd come back to finish me off. The thought of my baby being gone was too much for me mentally as well. I'd named her Camani and she was buried with a nice little tombstone. One thing I hated was the fact that I couldn't make it to Cam's funeral. I didn't even know where he was buried.

Coping was the only way I could describe how I was doing at the time. I'd had bouts of depression and oftentimes, I was so angry that all I could think about was revenge. One thing I knew was, I'd never ever be the same.

Rahz had killed my baby and my friend. At first, I was using Cam, but my feelings for him had become genuine once I was pregnant. He didn't have to go out of his way for me when she wasn't even his. He'd genuinely loved me, and I lost him that quick. Man, fuck my life. The one man who truly loved me was gone forever.

I was in pure misery, but life had to go on, right? Part of me wished Rahz had just killed me too. He was facing two first degree murder charges, and an attempted murder charge. I was so grateful that they'd charged him for my baby's murder as well. The story had made the news and Miami PD were on a manhunt.

Staring in the mirror, I had to admit that I looked pretty good after what I'd been through. The bruises and scars hadn't healed completely yet, but the doctors told me that they would in time. The irreversible damage to my heart and soul would never heal. That was something I knew for a fact.

At that point, I wasn't dealing with any men. I'd spoken to my boss and he knew what had happened, so I still had a job. He'd told me that I could come back whenever I wanted to. Fear made me want to hide in the house, but part of me wanted to get back out there. Besides, I needed the money. My medical bills were out the ass.

I'd been home for a whole week, but I refused to leave the house. The only thing I could see in my mind was Rahz following me somewhere and killing me. Yeah, he'd broken into my crib twice, but we had moved again. Now we lived in a gated community with security. We also had a very advanced alarm system. The locks had even been replaced by state of the art shit that Rahz couldn't possibly break into. The only place I felt safe was inside.

Sita was now working at Shadows and although she spent the first week at home with me, she had to return to work. Before she left she gave me the drill about the alarm and all that stuff like I didn't know.

"I'm sure nothing is going to happen to me. Besides, security won't let that nigga past the gate."

She gave me a sympathetic look. "You can't stay inside forever though cuz."

"I know, but once Rahz is taken care of, I can relax. Part of me hopes the cops shoot his ass instead of lockin' him up. Maybe this nigga'll go out with guns blazing."

"When you want them to kill a black man, they won't. If anything happens cuz, you already know what to do."

"Don't worry, I'll be fine."

She gave me a hug and left.

I just hoped what happened hadn't made national news because I didn't want Eddie or anybody to find out where I was. Being that I was just a black chick may have been a saving grace, because the news wasn't really making a buzz outside of Florida.

Yeah, I had a Facebook and Instagram page, but I used the name Ax (Xa spelled backwards) Butterfly. That was so I could lay low too. The thing was, Rahz knew what name I used on Facebook and he'd flooded my inbox the past twelve hours. What he didn't know was, I was told to contact the cops if he corresponded with me in any way. Hopefully they'd be able to use his social media pages to track his location.

That nigga had the nerve to send me the lyrics to "No Woman No Cry," by Bob Marley.

The next message was more sinister.

Rahz: Thought I killed you. Won't stop 'till I do.

Picking up the phone, I made a call to the head detective on my case.

"Detective Arnold," he answered.

"It's Xavia Perkins. Rahz inboxed me on Facebook. Y'all have to catch him. He's threatening to finish me off!"

"Calm down Miss Perkins."

"What do you mean, calm down? He killed my friend and my baby, and he tried to kill me. What makes you think he won't do exactly what he said. I can't even leave my home, because y'all haven't arrested his crazy ass yet."

"Miss Perkins, I understand your frustration..."

"Do you really? I don't think you really do. I'm just some black woman that you all don't give one damn about. Do you know how many times I called the cops before it went that far? You did nothing to stop it. Why would I think you'll do anything to stop it now?"

"Miss Perkins, look, we are doing everything we can to bring Rahzmir into custody. He's obviously not in the state anymore. We have some leads that prove he's in Texas. We're working with the authorities there to bring him in. You made us aware of his social media pages and we are monitoring them closely. Please, Miss Perkins, just let us do our job. Okay. Don't respond to him and please, let us know if anything else out of the ordinary happens."

Rolling my eyes, I ended the call and decided not to get back on Facebook. I just wanted my life to return to normal. I'd been diagnosed with Post Traumatic Stress Disorder as well as Anxiety. It was also hard as hell for me to sleep without sleeping pills. I'd been prescribed with so much medication, I could get so much money selling that shit on the street. The thing was, I needed it all.

* * *

Early the next morning my cell phone blared on my nightstand. When I checked the screen, I saw that it was a number I didn't recognize. My blood felt ice cold in my veins. Was it Rahz continuing his harassment? Something told me not to answer it, but I did.

"Miss Perkins? It's Detective Arnold. I'm calling to inform you that the suspect in your case was apprehended a few hours ago at Dallas Fort Worth Airport. He was planning to board a flight to Jamaica. They are going to extradite him back here next week to face his charges."

Damn, that was a relief and tears escaped my closed eyes. "Thank god. Thank you, Detective Arnold."

Then I thought about the fact that I'd have to face him if that shit went to trial. That was one thing that I was dreading, but I'd do whatever it took. If I couldn't get street justice, knowing that he'd never get out of prison was the next best thing.

"You're welcome. You never have to worry about him again. He's not getting a bond and the DA is going after the death penalty. The only way he can avoid death is by signing a plea for life with no chance of parole. In that case, he won't be put to death, but he won't ever get out. You won't have to testify against him in court if he takes the plea, so that's a good thing, right?"

"Yeah, I guess." I wanted him to die a slow, painful death, but I kept that shit to myself.

We hung up the phone and although they had him, I didn't really feel any better. I thought I would, but Cam and my baby girl were still gone. Rahz being behind bars wouldn't bring them back.

* * *

A few weeks later, I found myself trying to find some type of normalcy. I'd returned to my job and after getting a check, I decided to get my hair done. I was in the chair of my favorite stylist, Kimmie. She worked as a master stylist at a unisex salon called Hair, There and Everywhere.

Kimmie was almost finished with my silk press when I heard the chime on the door signaling that it had opened. Without even thinking about it, my attention went to the door. That's when I saw Duke walk in. His eyes widened when he saw me, but I looked away.

Once Kimmie was done, she turned my chair around so I could see my hair and passed me a handheld mirror.

"Oh yeah K, this shit is tight boo."

"Thanks love."

We hugged, and I went to pay at the front desk. I made sure to leave a twenty-dollar tip for my girl, booked another appointment in two weeks and left. Before I could make it to my car, I heard somebody call my name out behind me. Of course, it was Duke.

One thing I was sick and tired of was stalking ass niggas. Why didn't he just keep it moving with his married ass? I'd been through enough.

"Xa, c'mom, can you stop for a second."

Turning around with much attitude, I put my hand on my hips. "Why?"

"Yo, I heard 'bout what happened to you. Good to see that you a'ight ma. If you need anything, I'm here."

"Yeah, thanks," I walked off, but he was on my heels.

"It's been a long time…"

"Not long enough."

"Oh okay, you still mad."

"I ain't mad." I spun on my heels. "I've been through so much that I don't have time to be mad at you 'bout shit. You did lie to me, knowing that your ass is married. All you had to do was be truthful 'bout that shit. I'm grown and so are you. I ain't got time for games. I liked you a lot Duke, but that was then." Turning, I headed toward my car again.

"My number's the same if you wanna call me."

"You sure yo' wife won't mind?" My voice was sarcastic.

Duke sighed heavily. His body was so close to mine as I unlocked my door, I could feel his body heat. "I figured that would come up. We ain't really married."

"It don't even matter Duke. You wasn't my man then and you damn sure ain't my man now."

"You never gave me the chance to explain. I tried to call you, but you changed your number and shit."

"You don't have to explain shit to me, Duke. It's been almost a year since I saw you wit' your bitch, so I'm good."

"I met Ciara 'bout four years ago at a club and shit. At that time, I wasn't really diggin' her, but she was persistent. We started kickin' it and shit got real complicated..."

"Why are you tellin' me this shit? I told you I don't care."

He continued anyway. "We ain't married, but she's my fiancée. That shit really ain't by choice though..."

"Oh my god." Opening the car door, I tried to get in, but he pushed the door shut.

"Just listen to me," he pleaded.

"Hurry the fuck up. I got somewhere to go."

I turned to face him.

"Well, Tiffany's father is the Assistant DA for Miami Dade County. I ended up catching some charges. Her folks already didn't like me and shit. I got arrested like a year after I met Tiffany. Once her father caught wind of my charges, he couldn't wait to bribe me. His father admitted that he and his wife hated me, but they couldn't admit that to their daughter because she'd only cling to me and not deal with them. She's their only child, so they couldn't bear that. He explained that he would drop my charges due to lack of evidence if and only if I never hurt their daughter in any way. One of the conditions is, I have to marry her and never leave her for another woman. If anything, I thought they'd bribe me into leaving her alone. That shit caught me off guard, but I'd agree to anything for my freedom. When I met you, none of that shit mattered. When I saw you that night, I didn't know what to do. I wanted to tell you the truth, but I was so shocked. Now, I'm still willin' to risk it all. I miss the shit out of yo' ass. For real. You been through some crazy shit over the past year. I wanna make it better. I still want you. My feelings for old girl been gone. That was even way before I met you. It became clear that night you caught me, but I couldn't do shit. I didn't know what move to make next ma. Give me the word and I'll say fuck it. Old girl is history."

"I can't believe you actually tried to feed me some bullshit like that." Shaking my head, I opened my car door again.

"I'm tellin' the truth Xa. I swear. Shit, I'm not lyin' when I say I miss you. When I found out what happened to you, I wanted to kill that nigga my damn self. I wanted to reach out, but I ain't know where you was, or how to contact you. No more lies and no more games. Please, just let me back in. I wanna pick up where we left off. Give me a chance to prove myself. You won't regret it baby. I promise."

"You said I was nothing right to my face. Why the fuck would you want to do anything wit' me?"

His eyes were pleading with me. "I already told you what's up. You don't have to believe me, but it's the truth. At the time I was caught off guard and so, I said whatever I had to say. I didn't mean to hurt you or nothing."

Rolling my eyes, I started the car up. "Please don't flatter yourself. You didn't hurt me. If anything, you just showed me your true colors."

"It's a reason we ran into each other today ma. You gon' call me?"

"I'on know Duke. I might and I might not."

Pulling off, I looked in my rearview mirror at him just standing there. The thing was, I needed a sucka to get my pockets right. I'd make him sweat for a few days, but I planned to call.

His story did sound bogus, but I didn't really care about that. I already knew that he was good financially and whenever I was ready for the physical, I knew he was good on that. Getting back in the game wasn't on my agenda anytime soon. After what happened with Rahz, I would take my time meeting somebody new.

Chapter 12

Miami

2015

A few weeks later, I finally called Duke. Over the next couple months, we were inseparable. I told him he didn't have to drop his bitch. What was left of my heart wasn't built for love anymore anyway. I also wasn't ready to have sex again yet, so he needed someone to fulfill that need. Although he'd had the pussy before, he understood and didn't seem to be in a rush.

However, that shit didn't last too long. We'd gone out on like three dates before he felt that I owed him some ass. After what I'd been through, I thought he'd be more patient. At first, he made me think he would be.

We were in his Hummer and he couldn't keep his hands off me. Something told me that his bitch was at the crib, because he was hinting around about going to mine, or getting a room. His tongue was literally down my throat and I pushed him away.

"Umm, I'm sorry, Duke. I'on think I'm ready yet. Just take me home."

"A'ight, but damn ma. You act like you don't know me. I ain't just any nigga." He had an attitude and so did I.

"Didn't I say take me home? Shit. It don't matter if I know you or not. I ain't fuckin' ready."

Rolling my eyes, I adjusted my clothes as he drove off.

Something told me to leave Duke alone for good. Yeah, we had ran into each other again, but that didn't mean we had to deal with each other. So far, he'd only shown me over and over that his money wasn't enough to make me deal with him. I'd just been through some fucked up shit and all he could think about was getting some pussy. I'd never meet another man like Cam.

On the way to my apartment Duke was quiet as hell. The only communication between us was his facial expression when he looked up at me in the rearview mirror.

"What's wrong wit' yo' face?" As I asked, I screwed up mine.

"Nothing," he lied as he glanced up again.

Looking back, I noticed that it wasn't the cops. What was he so damn paranoid for?

"You know you lyin' like a mufucka."

Duke sighed. "Old girl is followin' us."

"Yo' bitch is followin' us?"

"Yeah," he simply said.

"What the fuck?"

"Don't worry..."

"Nigga, I ain't worried 'bout shit. That's you."

His nervousness was apparent, because his eyes kept darting from the rearview to his side mirror.

Shaking my head, I made a suggestion. "How 'bout you just pull over and face it. You said you ain't give a fuck and you'd leave her for me."

His face proved that he'd lied. Good thing he was the only one giving anything in the equation. Ohhh, I really hated him at that moment. Fuck him, his bitch, his freedom and his money.

"But you told me not to leave her for you 'cause you ain't ready."

That bitch was riding his ass and I was already fed up. We were only ten minutes from my spot and I wanted to deal with the drama before I got there. Suddenly, Duke hit the gas and we were going almost a hundred mph on the freeway. That nigga was acting like we were on a highspeed chase with the cops.

"Nigga, are you fuckin' crazy?" Holding on to the arm rest for dear life, I stared over at him.

"No, I'm tryna lose that bitch. Duck down."

"I ain't duckin' down for that bitch."

"That's easy for you to say."

"I don't give a shit who that bitch's daddy is, or whatever voodoo she got on your ass. That shit ain't got nothing to do wit' me nigga! Pull the fuck over and let me outta this gotdamn car!"

That nigga wasn't trying to hear shit I was saying. He got off on the next exit and turned down a desolate, side road. Headlights were behind us, although he'd been driving like a speed demon. That hoe was determined to catch him in some shit.

"I see that bitch won't give up."

"Damn." Perspiration was gathering on his forehead and the bridge of his nose.

"You really don't need to be cheatin' on that bitch, 'cause you obviously don't know how."

Next thing I knew, she rear-ended the car and it spun out twice before coming to rest on the shoulder of the road. When I realized that I was still alive, I opened the car door and got out. Then I walked over to that bitch's car, which was parked not too far from ours. She was still sitting behind the wheel with a smirk on her face.

Duke got out of the car too, but yelled out behind me. "What you doin'? Get back here!"

Man, fuck that shit.

That bitch rolled her window down ready to talk shit, but I didn't even waste my time with words. Instead, I grabbed that skinny bitch and pulled her out of the car through the window. She didn't know what the hell to do. My fists went to work on her ass and I tried to obliterate that bitch's face. Taking out all my hurt and pain on her, I tried my hardest to make that bitch feel it.

"Get the fuck off me hoe!" She screamed, frantically trying to swing back.

None of her wild swings landed because I was literally dragging that hoe. Before I could get her like I really wanted to, Duke pulled me off her. Her lip was bleeding, her face was getting lumpy and her eye was swelling.

"You still fuckin' with that bitch Duke!" Tears fell down her bruised cheeks. "You told me you was done wit' her ghetto ass!"

"Bitch, fuck you and Duke. Y'all can have each other." Walking off, I decided to do some crazy shit.

That nigga's Bentley was still running, and the keys were dangling from the ignition. He was so busy fussing with that bitch, he didn't notice me get behind the wheel until it was too late.

"Bring my fuckin' car back!" He yelled after me.

"Nigga, if you want this mufucka come get it and after you do leave me the fuck alone for good!"

After that was said, I rolled the window up and turned on the air. Damn, that shit was a smooth ass drive. Although that bitch had hit that shit, there was no damage done. That shit was well-built. I'd just enjoy pushing that shit for the moment. There was no doubt that Duke would be back to get it. The thing was, I wasn't about to wait for him and that bitch to work shit out. My ass was out of that mufucka. I'd already beat her dumb ass for trying to kill us. All the fucking money in the world wouldn't make me want to deal with that drama. Fuck that.

* * *

Not even two hours later, Duke was calling talking about he was coming to pick his car up.

"You better not have that bitch bring you over here, or I'm gon' kill both y'all mufuckas."

"Man, kill that bullshit you talkin'. You ain't gon' kill shit and, no she ain't bringin' me. I'm takin' a fuckin' Uber."

"Well, yo' keys will be in the front seat. Don't bother comin' to my door, or tryna fuck wit' me again. I'm done wit' you. I should've been done the moment you decided to shoot a nigga while I waited in the car. Fuck you and that anorexic, mannequin lookin' bitch! Y'all can both kiss my fuckin' ass! Bye Duke! Have a nice life wit' yo' skeleton!"

After I ended the call, I went outside and put his car keys in the driver's seat. After that I went back inside, locked the door, set the alarm and went back to bed. The way I saw it, that was one less problem for me to worry about.

* * *

Over the next two weeks, I worked doubles and did whatever I had to do to pay my high ass bills. Our rent was twelve hundred dollars a damn month. Sita was also working at the lounge as a waitress. She seemed to like doing that more than her last job.

I'd even sold the whip Cam gave me just to have some extra cash on hand. The fact was, I was literally tired of men, but I needed a sucker to milk. I didn't have the desire to fuck anybody though, so that would make it harder. A nigga would give without me fucking him, but that shit wouldn't last for too long.

On a rare day off, me and Sita hit up a club called The Diamond Bar. We had been on the dancefloor for at least an hour twerking and working up a sweat. It was time to hit the bar and when we did, the owner approached me.

"You are so beautiful," he told me breathlessly as if the sight of me had taken the air right out of his lungs.

"Thank you."

He introduced himself to me as Davon and We exchanged numbers. He called me first of course and we went on a few dates. The thing was, he showed signs of falling in love early on and I hadn't even kissed that nigga.

See, Davon was an older cat. He was about thirty-two and owned a few businesses in Miami. That was impressive, but something about him threw me off. For instance, on our second date he was trying too hard. He kept telling everybody at the restaurant that I was his woman and he was going to marry me.

Umm, we'd only known each other for two weeks and I wasn't planning on marrying his ass, or anybody else. Davon was nice looking with almond toned skin, a nice, athletic build and sexy brown eyes with long lashes. However, he seemed too attached to me too soon. It was clear that he was looking for a younger woman to marry and bear his children. He made that obvious in our many

176 | A Heartless Goon Snatched My Soul

conversations. The straw that broke the camel's back was when he kept pushing the issue on his way to take me home after our third date.

"Look, I got a lot to offer a woman. You don't seem to be interested."

He was obviously out of the loop because he didn't know about me from the news. I guess I also looked different being that I wasn't all busted up and bruised. Not offering him an explanation as to why, I just told him straight, no chaser.

"I'm not interested in doing anything with you other than enjoying your company for now."

"Well, I don't want to waste any time Xa. I mean, I want to find a wife and make some babies."

The laughter escaped before I could hold it back. "I met you two weeks ago. Slow down. I ain't ready for marriage or babies anytime soon."

"It's funny to you?" Shaking his head, he continued. "I pour my heart out and it's funny to you?"

"Nah, actually it's fuckin' scary, not funny."

He didn't say anything else after that. Fifteen minutes later, he pulled up in front of my building and I got out without even saying bye. We kept in touch, but I knew that nothing would ever come of that.

* * *

My luck with the opposite sex would soon change for the better. On a busy Saturday night at

Shadows, I happened to be serving a table with two very handsome men. One was named Dutch and his fine, bronze toned ass kept right on staring and smiling at me.

Next thing I knew, he was clearly flirting. "Damn ma, where yo' ring at? I know some nigga done snatched yo' fine ass up and locked you down. And if so, you need to drop that loser. If you were mine, you wouldn't have to work." With that said, he licked his nice, thick lips.

"No man, no ring, no husband and I choose to work," I told him before sashaying away.

Making sure to put an extra twist in my hips, I didn't have to look back to know that he was watching. My back was literally burning. When I got back to the table his homeboy was gone.

"So, can you take a minute to sit down and talk to me." He flashed that winning smile of his.

Straight white teeth, flawless, good looks and his charm had me interested.

"I can't. I'm on the clock and I have other tables."

He reached in his pocket, pulled out a gold billfold and peeled off a couple hundred dollar bills. After putting them on the table, he peered up at me.

"Is that enough for a minute?"

Rolling my eyes, I salivated over the money, but played it off. Then he peeled off another hundred and another.

"Okay, you're doin' too much." A smile crept up on my face though.

"It's more where that come from."

"Well, I ain't for sale."

"And I ain't tryna buy you. I just know that time is money." He gestured toward the chair in front of him. "So, you gon' give me a minute, or what?"

Looking around the busy restaurant, I knew that my boss would be pissed if he saw me. But, a minute of sitting wouldn't hurt.

"You have exactly sixty seconds." Before sitting down, I grabbed the hundreds and put them in my apron.

He grinned at me and my icy heart skipped ten beats.

* * *

The sound of the doorbell woke me up from a peaceful slumber. Putting the cover over my head, I hoped Sita would get it. When it kept on ringing, I knew that she wasn't. Part of me wished they'd just leave, but that was not the case. Whoever it was decided to start knocking like the damn police.

"Shit, I'm comin'! Damn!"

Looking through the peephole, I saw that it was Rob. What the fuck was he doing here? Sita didn't fuck with him anymore.

I went ahead and opened the door.

"Hey Rob."

"Hey Xa. How you holdin' up?"

"I'm makin' it."

"You should've told me what was up with that nigga Rahz. I would've murked his ass." The anger was clear in his eyes as he continued. "Cam was my partna, man. I can't believe how that shit went down."

Really not wanting to talk about that, I nodded. "You lookin' for Sita?"

"Yeah, she here?"

"I just woke up. Did you see her car?"

"Yeah, it's out there."

"A'ight. Is she expecting you?"

Shit, he was no better than Rahz for choking her out that time.

"Nah, but we have been talkin'. She ain't tell you that."

"Nah, she didn't and just 'cause y'all been talkin' don't make it cool for you to just be poppin' up."

His eyes reverted down. "Look, I know she told you 'bout what happened, but it wasn't like that. It's two sides to every story and..."

"Save it." I put my hand up. "I really couldn't less about your side of the story. You wait out here while I go get her."

It was better to be safe than sorry. I'd learned that shit the hard way.

Closing the door, I locked it and made my way down the hall. I knocked on Sita's bedroom door, but she didn't say anything?

"Sita, you in there?"

There was still no response, so figuring that she was asleep, I opened the door.

"Aww shit!" Sita scooted away from Cherrie, who was feasting away on her pussy.

I mean, that bitch was going in. Her whole damn face was in there. When she looked up at me, she licked her wet lips.

Turning around, I told Sita, "Uh, I'm sorry for barging in. I thought you were sleep. Rob is at the door for you."

With that said, I closed the door and walked off. I hadn't told Sita about that shit with Cherrie and I hadn't seen her in a minute. That was the way I wanted to keep it, because that bitch was trying it when she did that shit. It didn't matter that the bitch could eat the hell out of a pussy, I still wanted to kill her for violating me.

Chapter 13

Miami

2016

Some time passed before I got a call from the detective to let me know that Rahz had taken the plea deal.

"He'll never get out, so although he didn't receive the death penalty, you can be relieved that he'll never hurt you again. It'll be a while before he is sent to prison, but I thought you'd like to know that you don't have to testify against him."

I thanked him for calling me, and then hung up. Relief wasn't what I was feeling once the call was over. Yeah, he couldn't hurt me again, but I wanted him dead. I'd been told that Rahz's defense lawyer would make me look like a whore who fucked Rahz for money and played him against Cam. I wasn't afraid to go through that, for him to get the death penalty. That nigga deserved to die for the shit he'd done to me.

The only thing that made me smile was the thought of seeing Dutch later. He was so damn sexy, charismatic and smart. Not only that, but his pockets were deep as fuck. He was Mexican and black and his father, who was from Mexico, ran a drug smuggling cartel.

When I saw his white Bugatti pull up to pick me up for our first date, I was feeling like things were finally looking up for a bitch. As I stepped in and took in the white interior and mink rugs, my pussy was instantly wet. Shit, I hadn't felt any stirring down there in a while. Hmm, maybe the money smell in the car had awakened the beast.

Still, I held out and made that nigga wait. Besides, he hadn't spent any real money yet. By our third date, he was spending his funds like water. He'd even give me money to pay my bills and it had only been a couple months since we met.

"Why are you spoilin' me so much?"

We were Facetiming, and he kept right on smiling at me. He was in New York, which was where his mother was originally from. They owned a hot ass penthouse in Manhattan and I was dying to see it for myself.

The trip to New York with Rahz had never happened and I really wanted to go. I wasn't one to beat around the bush though. I knew that if he wanted me to come there, he'd ask. Then he did.

"You're worth spoilin'. I knew that from the moment I saw you. Then the fact that you ain't some thot makes me wanna do it even more. I'm not gonna tell you what's gonna happen ma. I like to show and prove. See, my plans are to make you fall in love wit' a nigga. It's time for you to see how a real man treats a woman. I wanna not only spoil you, but I wanna pamper you and nurture your spirit. I wanna be the one to help you heal from the past. I won't rush it though. How 'bout I fly you out here, so we can spend some time together. I won't be back to Miami anytime soon, and I miss you. I can't even lie."

"Are you a mind reader? I was waitin' for you to invite me. I gotta admit I miss you too."

He chuckled. "If you wanted to come out here why didn't you say something?"

"I ain't wanna push myself on you."

"Hmm, it's nothing I want more than for you to push yourself on me. I want you so bad, I can taste that shit. When you ain't around, I can smell the sweet scent of your hair and perfume. I can feel your soft hands on my face. I'm ready to feel something else, for real, ma. I'm ready to make you feel something else."

So, we made plans for me to fly out to New York City in two weeks.

Damn, he was so different than any man I knew. At the time, I was twenty-one. My twenty second birthday was just a month away. A lot of time had passed since what happened with Rahz, but it was still hard for me to let go of the pain. That inner voice told me not to get my feelings involved regardless of how much game he spat.

My soul hadn't returned yet and so, it became easier and easier for me to use men. My only condition was, I wasn't willing to deal with any drama a nigga brought to the equation. If it came down to it, I'd do whatever I had to do to make my own money.

The tips I made at Shadows were good, especially on the weekends. However, I had developed very expensive taste. That shit just wasn't enough. So, I decided to sell my prescription meds. They were endless, so why not make some money. Most of my clientele were employees, or regulars at Shadows, so it was easy to do. I had enough Xanax and OxyContin to make money to take care of myself. The only problem was, I took those Xans like candy myself.

* * *

"My flight's been delayed." Pissed and impatient, I explained the situation to Dutch over the phone.

"How long?" He sounded sympathetic.

"Until further notice. They said something about the weather. It a thunderstorm here."

"Well, you do know it's Hurricane season. I wanna see you so bad though. Don't worry. You gon' get here if I have to send my driver for you."

"I'm sure I'll be in the sky in no time." Well, at least I hoped so.

Popping a Xan, I put the prescription bottle in my purse. I wasn't worried about getting though security with it since it was in my name.

"Well, I'm anxious as fuck."

"I can't wait to see you either."

"That's good to hear." He chuckled. "Just don't get frustrated and leave the airport. I gotta see you. I can't take it no more, ma. You got my head all fucked up and I ain't even had the pleasure of tastin' you yet. Promise me you won't leave. If you do, let me know what's up, so I can figure out another way to get you here."

"I won't leave, I promise."

We talked a little longer and then he told me to call him back when I knew something. After about two hours, I was finally boarding the plane. Dutch had paid for my first-class round trip ticket. After experiencing first class once, I had to demand it. Once when Duke took me to Vegas, we flew first class. It was no problem, because I didn't even have to ask Dutch. He was the one who booked my flight. I laid back, sipped some Chardonnay and relaxed.

Dutch told me that he was waiting at baggage claim when I called him. We'd just landed and were getting off the plane. My ass was hungry although I'd had a meal of steak, broccoli and a baked potato.

"I can't wait to see yo' pretty ass," he told me.

"I'm on my way." In no time I did spot him.

His back was turned to me and, so I crept up on him. Standing there for a second, I waited for him to turn around. I knew that he'd either feel, or smell me behind him, since he said my scent was embedded in his memory.

"There's my baby." He was smiling so damn hard when he saw me. "I smelled yo' perfume."

My breath caught in my throat. His wavy fro was done in a bunch of small box braids and he had a fresh shape up. The braids were so fresh and tight they made his sexy eyes look even more slanted. Damn, Dutch was finer than a mufucka. I had to admit that shit. My eyes went straight to his thick ass lips. As much as I tried to defy it, I wanted to kiss them.

"You look even better than you did last time I saw yo' sexy ass." He pulled me into him for an embrace.

Then he finally covered my lips with his. Our passionate kiss lingered, and the many by standers watched our public display of affection.

"Mmm, what's that perfume called? It smells too damn good." His face was buried in my neck, inhaling.

Tingles traveled all over my body and my skin overheated as butterflies fluttered in the pit of my stomach.

"It's called Noa." My voice was seductive and low.

He finally separated from me and smiled, flashing that one deep dimple.

"You ain't nervous is it? You safe wit' me baby?"

His smile seemed so genuine, but I questioned my logic. Yeah, I'd gone out with him before, but you'd think I'd be more careful after the shit I'd been through. What if he was psycho as fuck too? Then again, what was the probability of me being raped, or almost killed again?

Returning his smile, I said, "It's cool. My cousin Sita got all the info on you she needs. If I don't get back off that plane in four days, she gon' be on it."

"You're smart and fine as fuck. I love it bae."

Finally, my luggage rolled in front of me. After that we were out. He led me to a cocaine white E-class big body Benz and it was laid baby. That mufucka was sitting on 24's and had all the perks of a luxury vehicle.

Once we were in the car, I took in that new car smell. I wanted to ask if he'd just gotten it, but I didn't want to sound too impressed.

"Can you drive a stick?" He asked as he shifted the gears on the way out of the airport's parking lot.

"Nah, but I can ride one," I blatantly blurted out.

"Damn, you know I'm hard as fuck right now, right?"

My flirtatious giggle filled the intimate space.

"I'm sure you are."

"Confident. That's that shit I'm talkin' 'bout."

Letting out a yawn, I leaned back in my seat. "You tired?"

"A little. I had a few glasses of wine on the plane." Leaving out the Xanax, I figured I'd keep that shit to myself.

"You can relax. We'll be at the spot in twenty minutes if traffic ain't too bad. When we get to the spot, I'll call my personal masseuse Christine to come give you a massage."

"Do I have the option of a man?"

Looking over at me, he sternly said, "Hell no. I'm the only man who gon' be feelin' on yo' fine ass while you here." The sultry look he flashed my way made me instantly hot

Laughing, I stretched and put my seat back. "Well, I'm gon' take a power nap."

"Help yourself. The seats warm up. It's a lil' nippy here and shit. I know you used to that tropical weather. I love New York, but I can't get used to this cold shit."

It was October and about sixty degrees. I was used to that growing up in Atlanta though. It often got cold and it could get very windy. Soon we were at the high rise where Dutch's hot ass penthouse was.

As soon as we got there Dutch kissed me and told me that he had to step out for a couple hours for some business.

"I promise you I won't be gone long. It's no way I invited you here not to spend any time wit' you. After this it's all about you." His hand was under my chin affectionately.

Uggh, I hated the fact that all I could feel was a physical connection to him. My greedy side was thinking about money, not giving a fuck that he was saying all the right shit. That had already got me in a vulnerable position with Rahz. He'd said all the right shit, but could not be trusted.

What if Dutch was just like him or worse? Maybe I should've thought about that before I boarded that plane.

"Okay." With a nod and a pout, I hugged him tight before he left.

Giving myself a tour, I saw that the penthouse took up the entire fourteenth floor of the building. It was near Greenwich Village and was really nice. I looked around and there was nothing but white people roller blading, bicycling or walking their dogs. It was so peaceful and far from the New York stereotype. No one acknowledged one another with a wave or nod, like down south, but it was cool just the same.

I'd been told earlier by Dutch that his mother had decorated the penthouse. Dutch was really the only one who was ever there though. He said although she was from there, his mother rarely visited New York.

Staring at the revolving glass doors, I spotted a tall, slim doorman. He was white and wore a blue uniform with red trim. He even had on a hat to match. He looked silly to me, but was all part of New York's scene.

The driver, Henry was taking me out to get that massage that Dutch had promised me. See, although his masseuse made house calls, it was best for me to go to her at the time.

After I was pampered and relaxed, we returned to the penthouse. Henry made small talk with the doorman and then we headed to the elevator. When the number fourteen blinked the elevator stopped and the doors opened.

The penthouse was laid. Thick, plush, cream colored carpet donned the floors and modern, African art decorated the walls. Chic, colorful furniture created the perfect aura of Feng-sui. I even loved the kitchen and I hated cooking. Maybe if I had a kitchen like that shit would be different.

"Are you hungry Miss," a brown skinned older man in a dark suit asked.

I found out later that he was Celesto, the butler.

"Kinda, my name is Xa."

The man's brown eyes were gentle although he was huge in size. He had to be at least six three and over two hundred pounds.

"As you know, I work for Mr. Dutch. I'm his butler and chef. Whatever, you fancy, I can prepare." He had a slight French accent to match. Maybe he was Haitian.

"Mr. Dutch will be here shortly."

There was a blank expression on his face and he was all business. Soon we were talking like we were old friends. It didn't take as much as I thought it would for him to feel comfortable with me.

"Well, you're the chef and I love to eat. Surprise me."

The breathtaking view from the huge window in the kitchen had my attention.

"Feel free to make yourself at home. I'll prepare a good lunch for you."

"Thanks. This is my first time in New York, so I'm so ready for Dutch to take me sight-seeing. I've already given myself a tour. This place is incredible, but I'm ready to get out."

"No problem at all and you're going to love it here. I'm from Haiti, but I've been living here in New York since I was eight years old. There's no other place I'd rather call my second home. Where are you from?"

"I'm from Atlanta originally, but I live in Miami. That's where I met Dutch."

"Oh yes, I've visited both. I must admit that I like Atlanta better although I like Miami's beaches. New York is probably a lot more fast paced than what you're used to, but I'm sure you can handle it." He smiled at me and I relaxed. Finally, a facial expression.

After that I walked off to the master bath to take a shower. After that I changed into some jeans and a thin, red sweater. Now I had an excuse to wear the tan brown Ugg's Dutch had bought for me. They definitely couldn't be worn in Miami.

When I returned to the kitchen I saw that Celesto was preparing some piping hot chicken fajitas with rice. There were even fresh tortillas, guacamole and salsa on the side. He put my plate in front of me and my mouth watered.

"Celesto, this looks so good." One thing I could say was I loved Mexican food.

"Enjoy. Henry has left to pick Mr. Dutch up. He'll be here shortly."

He left me to enjoy my meal all by my lonesome. That shit was so good that I wanted seconds, so I filled my plate up again. After I ate, I washed my dishes and decided to watch some TV until Dutch got there.

About thirty minutes later he walked in the room and I forgot about anything else. His cologne made an entrance before his fine ass did.

"Hey mami." As he plopped down beside me I tried to play it cool, but I wanted to sop his fine ass up with a damn biscuit. That nigga smelled so scrumptious.

"From here on out, I'm only goin' to be spendin' time wit' you. Business can wait."

"Promise."

"I promise." His eyes penetrated mine.

Leaning over, he gave me a sweet peck on the lips. That must've not been enough, because he dipped back in for a more passionate kiss. When he pulled away, he sucked softly on my bottom lip.

"I know y'en come all the way here to sit around the crib, so get dressed." He playfully slapped me on the ass.

He didn't have to tell me twice. Getting up, I gave him a sexy look.

"Just promise we'll hit that Jacuzzi up when we get back."

"Hmm." Licking his sexy lips, he added, "Anything you want, wit' yo' sexy ass."

We ended up at a spot that had open mic nights. Any poet, rapper, spoken word artist, singer, musician, etc. could display their talent for an audience.

My ass ended up getting up to hit the mic. I couldn't sing, rap or no shit like that, but I often wrote poetry. It was therapeutic and was one of the things my therapist recommended for me to get over my trauma. All my poetry wasn't dark though. I had some shit that was a little more lighthearted. Not only did I keep my talent to myself, but I also kept the dark poems a secret. They were only for me.

Having a few drinks in me, I felt a little more open and brave than usual. Why not share? They were all strangers, except for Dutch. The way he beamed at me when I stood to walk on stage proved that he didn't care what I said. He was just happy to see me having a good time.

Grabbing the mic, I cleared my throat. "Hi, I'm Xa, and I'm gonna spit a poem I wrote a while back."

The crowd gave me their undivided attention.

"I see you lookin' out the corner of your eye. Lookin' all cute, tryna front like you shy. You lickin' your lips, and lookin' all mean. Wonderin' if you can get in these jeans..." I sang that part like Genuwine before I continued. The crowd went wild with hoots, whistles and claps. "Don't be intimidated, just ask me if I got a man, instead of assuming that I do. If I'm lookin'... who knows... it could be you. But you standin' there, still just peepin' my style. Maybe you got a girl and she ain't gave you none in a while. You just lookin' for a one night stand, and you'll never leave yo' baby mama. Your truck is parked outside. It's the black rimmed up Hummer. I'm feelin' you too, but I ain't the one to make the first move. I start swayin' to the beat as you discreetly watch me groove. Now I'm frustrated 'cause it's a quarter past two. I walk to the restroom three times just to catch a glimpse of you. Why won't you say something? Can't you feel my lust? I can't help it. I ain't that bitch, but leavin' wit' you is a must. But, you keep watchin', never uttering a word, not a gesture, or a clue. What the fuck is wrong wit' you? Now it's after three and the party's windin' down. The lights come on and I quickly look around. It's hot as hell and we make a beeline to the door. Me and my girls were lit and worked the floor. But, the entire night, there was one thing on my mind. The fine nigga in the corner wit' the swag, wearin' all that shine. Stomach's rumblin', we stop at Ihop before goin' to the crib. All them drinks at the bar put a dent in my ribs. Then I spot yo' fine ass chillin' at a booth in the back. You got a look on yo' face now, like, yeah, I found her. Then I hear it, a voice low and deep. "Come here ma, you lookin' all sweet." We converse for a few and everything is cool. You tell me you work full time and go to school. Just my type... fine and ambitious. Bitches checkin' you out and I wanna kill them bitches. We exchange numbers, and everything is tight. This all went down on Ladies' Night."

Man, everybody was on their feet clapping, and snapping their fingers. When I got back to the table with Dutch, he had an amazed expression on his face.

"Damn, y'en tell me you're a poet. That shit was hot. You got the voice to rap too. You ever thought of doin' that?"

"Honestly, no. It's just a hobby. I write poetry, but I don't really perform. Shit, I figured I'm in New York. Nobody knows me but you... so why not?

He smiled. "Yeah, but people had their cell phones out recording. That shit might go viral."

Oh shit. That was one thing I didn't want to happen at all. Ignoring that prospect, we continued to enjoy each other's company before hitting up a club. We danced all up on each other, and the sensations that traveled over my body when he touched me had me weak. Shit, I was still a woman despite what had been done to me, and I had the desire for some dick.

Chapter 14

New York

2016

Me and Dutch got back to the penthouse after grabbing some good food at a late-night diner. The first thing I did was take a shower to wash off the sweat I'd worked up dancing on that fine ass nigga. He came in to check up on me.

"You tired yet bae?" He asked.

The shower's door hid my nakedness from his eyes, but he'd see all of me soon enough.

"No. I'm wired," I admitted.

"Okay. I'm gon' take a shower in the other bathroom. I'll be in the Jacuzzi waitin' for you."

That nigga was really letting shit flow the way it should. It was like he was in no rush and he would rather savor the moment of seeing me in all my naked glory. He was definitely getting some of this good pussy for being so patient with me. That throb between my thighs started again. It was a sign that I at least could still feel something, even if it wasn't love.

Dutch and I may not have fucked yet, but we'd damn sure had enough phone sex. We'd even did some freaky Facetime sessions. There was nothing like the real thing and I was actually glad that my sexual desires had resurfaced. There were times when my anxiety and PTSD bothered me, but for the most part, I was trying to get back to some form of normal. One thing I didn't want was to end up in some psych ward.

Like he said he'd be, Dutch was waiting for me in the Jacuzzi. There was a fat blunt dangling from his lips. The smoke wafted around him, making a thick, fragrant cloud.

"Mmm, that shit smells good."

Looking back, he flashed a sly smile. "Damn, you gon' make me do some shit to yo' ass you'll never forget. You gon' write poems about that shit."

With a laugh, I lowered my butt naked ass into the warm water. The jets caressed my skin and as I scooted closer to him, he put his arm around me. Then he passed me the blunt before pouring some champagne into two glasses with his free hand. He didn't move from his position with me in the process. Even that man's deodorant smelled good.

Passing me a glass, he shook his head. "You smell like heaven woman. Got my head swimmin'."

"That might just be the weed." I took a sip of the sweet champagne.

He laughed and stared at me. The look in his eyes was intense and the laughter was gone. "Nah, that's all you."

"Well, thank you."

He leaned over and started kissing my neck. I shivered as my pleasure zones were awakened. If I wasn't in that Jacuzzi, I'd have a pool of juice under me.

"I wanna eat yo' pussy so fuckin' bad." His hand was on my thigh, reaching up slowly. Then his finger was inside me, exploring my depths. "Damn, that pussy's tight."

"You wanna eat it, so eat it." My eyes challenged him, letting him know that I'd had enough of the talking. It was time for some action.

His tongue was on my breasts and then he started to suck on my nipples. He stood and lifted me up out of the water. Without bothering to dry either of us off, he carried me to his bed and laid me down gently.

My anticipation grew as he positioned himself between my thighs and blew on my hardened clit.

In no time his warm, wet tongue was on my clitoris. He started with a gentle lick that turned into a gentle suck. Switching between the two, he added more pressure, causing me to grind into his mouth. The sensations were taking over every sense in my body.

"Mmm… Dutch…"

That nigga ate the hell out of my pussy. Shit, I thought Duke was good at that shit. That nigga Dutch was fucking amazing. He spread my lips with his fingers and concentrated on sucking my swollen clit.

"Fuck!" I screamed out as he grabbed my ass and pulled me into his mouth.

That nigga was doing all types of tongue tricks. He'd go up, down, around and around, do figure eights, and lock his lips around my clit as he suckled gently. The entire time he'd make these loud, sexy ass, slurping noises.

"Mmm... yo' pussy tastes like cotton candy." As he continued to suck, his pointer and middle fingers pushed against my G-spot.

My pussy muscles pulsated against his fingers and I felt a powerful orgasm rock me.

"Fuck! Yessss Dutch!" Holding on to the back of his head, I twerked my pussy in his face, working just as hard as him for another nut.

A bitch was being greedy for that shit and Dutch didn't mind at all. He kept right on eating my pussy until what I had left of a soul literally drifted from my body. My eyes were closed as I whimpered weakly in pleasure. I had to have cum at least six times already and a bitch was spent. My insides were so gooey and wet that all I wanted was his dick buried deep inside me.

"Fuck me...." I moaned as he continued licking and sucking on my sensitive clit.

After I came once again, he finally came up for air. As he kissed me, he reached over to grab a condom from the nightstand drawer. He didn't even break our kiss as he ripped it open. His dick was a nice length and girth. My thing was, it was super thick. That was what I liked.

Dutch slowly slid inside my wetness and his eyes rolled back as he looked down at me. The power of the pussy, yasss! Clenching my muscles, I grabbed that nigga's ass and put the vice grip on that dick.

"Ugghhh... damn..." He stared at me in amazement. "Yo' pussy's better than I imagined. Fuck!"

Picking up the pace, he put my legs on his shoulders and literally dug my pussy out. I was so wet my pussy was popping like some hot grease. Dutch was literally fucking the pure shit out of me. When he picked me up and leaned me against the wall, he spread my legs so wide that it was like I was in a standing Chinese split. My toes hit the wall. It was a good thing I was flexible.

"Ohhh... shit!" That nigga's dick was so far up in my guts, I couldn't help but scream. "Fuck Dutch!"

"Mmm... Xa... throw it back... ma... Hell yeah, just like that!"

He put his forehead against mine and our lips joined. His hands were around my ankles and that nigga was grinding up inside me like his life depended on making me nut again. Staring right into his eyes, I did exactly what he said and threw the pussy back at him. Holding on to his muscular ass cheeks, I used my pussy control to suck him in even deeper.

Dutch's eyes widened. "Get yo' dick baby!"

"It's mine?" I asked breathlessly.

"All yours... arggghhh... shit!" His forehead wrinkled, and he bit down on his bottom lip.

Damn, he had some good ass dick. That shit was making me feel like I could only fuck him. I didn't need anybody else, because after his dick, theirs would only seem mediocre. I'd had my share of sexual encounters, but Dutch was going where no other man had gone before. That nigga was digging in uncharted land.

"Uhhh... yo' dick's too good! Fuck!"

"That's that pussy ma..." He told me breathlessly.

Finally releasing my legs from his grasp, Dutch picked me up against, turned me around and made me lean against the dresser. Then he lifted one of my legs and placed my foot on the dresser.

"Arch yo' back... Mmm hmm... just like that."

My muscles pulled him in when he reentered me. The position he had me in made it so that my pussy was wide the fuck open.

"Oh yeah... argghhh..." He groaned into my neck. "Shit Xa!"

Looking back, I watched my ass cheeks jiggle as his glistening dick moved in and out of me.

"This is my pussy now!" He held on to my waist tightly and stared grinding in deep circles.

My muscles jerked and twitched, squeezing his dick for dear life. Dutch was stirring that shit up like coffee.

"Yesss, yesss, this is yo' pussy!" That nigga slapped my ass cheeks and then started kneading them like dough.

We came hard as hell together and I had to close my eyes, letting the sweet climax take me to another place. When I opened my eyes, and looked up in the mirror, he was staring at me.

"You look so pretty when you cum. I just wanna look at your ass. Mmm, you make the sexiest face when I go deep." His lips were on my neck.

That shit made me shiver.

"I'on wanna rush you Xa, but you gon' be mine. That's a fuckin' promise."

He slid out of me and walked off to go the bathroom. My legs were so damn weak, I could hardly make it back to the bed. A bitch had to sit down before I went to wash my pussy. The lips were swollen as hell, so I knew that shit would hurt.

Dutch gently washed me down and we snuggled to go to sleep in the spooning position.

"Sleep tight gorgeous," he whispered in my ear before he started snoring lightly.

In less than a minute, I was out too.

* * *

Me and Dutch had been fucking nonstop, but over the next couple days we packed a lot in. I'd seen the Statue of Liberty, the Empire State Building and Times Square. There had even been a light snow, but it didn't really stick. Just seeing the snow flurries were enough for me. It hardly ever snowed in Atlanta and of course, it never snowed in Miami.

We ate at some of the most luxurious five-star restaurants in the city, saw *The Color Purple* on Broadway and went shopping on Fifth Avenue. I had enough name brand shit to fill two walk-in closets. The pussy must've been A one because that nigga was spending money like water. How was I going to get back on the plane with all that shit?

We only drunk the finest and smoked the highest grade Kush. Not only was Dutch a big spender, but he also knew how to treat a woman. He opened doors and pulled out chairs. He'd even rubbed my feet after a night out in heels. We weren't officially together, but he liked to cuddle. Although I thought Rahz had taken any ability I had to feel, I was feeling something.

Still, I had to be careful. My soul was empty, and my heart was still shattered. As much as I wanted to let Dutch in, I had to be realistic. What were the chances of me finding true love? If anything, the odds were against me and I had to remember that. The memories of Rahz assaulting me resurfaced as if it was just yesterday. I woke up in a cold sweat, breathing hard as hell. My chest was hurting as if I was having a damn heart attack.

Dutch held me close to him as he rubbed my hair. "Xa, you okay baby?"

His voice was soothing and as the tears spilled down my face, I thought about it. I hadn't taken a Xanax since I got off the plane. That shit was an anxiety attack. As I did what my therapist said and took deep breaths, I calmed down.

"Yes, I'm okay," I whispered.

"What was that? Did you have a bad dream?" Dutch asked.

"Uh, yeah... it was a bad dream." I lied.

"It's okay baby." Holding me close to him, he continued to rub my hair until I finally fell back asleep.

* * *

It was nine o' clock in the morning when I groggily opened my eyes. Dutch was getting dressed as if he was going somewhere. He'd told me that it was all about me, so I was wondering what was going on.

"You leavin'?" I didn't want him too. Besides, I was going back to Florida the next day.

"I'm sorry ma, something came up." He kissed my cheek. "I gotta step out, but it'll only be for a few hours. I promise."

"Get back in the bed." I pouted and lifted the cover up on his side.

He smiled, slid his hand under the cover and palmed my naked ass.

"As much as I want to, I can't. When I get back I'll make sure you enjoy yo' last night here. If it was up to me, you'd stay."

"I wish I could."

"You can."

Hoping he'd put his business aside and stay there with me, I kept trying. "But I don't want you to go. What am I gonna do while you're gone?"

He stood up and leaned over to kiss me again. I guess morning breath didn't matter to him. "I'll be back by one. You can do whatever you want. I'll get Celesto to cook you some breakfast. You need to build yo' strength back up. I know I took a lot of it outta you last night..."

"And this morning," I added.

He chuckled. "Later baby girl."

Waving sadly as he left the room, I fell back against the pillow and sighed. After popping a Xan, I fell back to sleep.

The sound of a knock at the door woke me up about an hour later.

"Yes!" I called out.

"Miss Xa, your breakfast is ready," Celesto said.

"Thank you Celesto!"

Not really feeling hungry, I got up anyway. After brushing my teeth and washing my face, I helped myself to waffles, turkey bacon, eggs, grits and fresh brewed coffee. As usual, Celesto's cooking was the shit.

After breakfast, I took a long shower, got dressed and sat down to watch some TV. I had to catch up on my favorite ratchet reality shows. When it was after one o' clock, I started to wonder where Dutch was. I called his cell phone, but it went to the voicemail.

Getting up, I went to find Celesto. He was in the kitchen cleaning up.

"Celesto, have you heard from Dutch? He said he'd be here by now. It's almost two."

"No, I haven't, but don't worry. I'm sure he'll be here soon." He went back to cleaning and I went back to the sitting room.

It was hard for me to just sit around and wait. After calling Dutch's phone again, I left a message. Four o' clock rolled around, and I still hadn't heard from him. By the time I called him again, it didn't even ring, but went straight to the voicemail.

By ten o' clock that night I was on panic mode. Celesto was trying to play it off as nothing, but I wasn't convinced. Knowing the risks that came with his lifestyle, I couldn't help but think the worst. What if he'd been killed or something?

Damnit, where the fuck was he? I didn't know what to think. After one in the morning, I was sick of calling. That nigga probably had a main bitch in New York and that was where he was. In that case, why the fuck did he invite me there?

I found a bottle of Pinot Grigio in the kitchen, rolled a blunt from Dutch's stash and popped a Xanax. About an hour later, I drifted off to sleep. When I woke up at six am, the penthouse was empty. Even Celesto wasn't there. I checked my phone to see if Dutch had called me back. Shit, there were no missed call or messages. Fuck! My flight back to Miami was eight o' clock that night.

When I dialed Dutch's number, I got the voicemail again. At that point, I was frustrated. "Dutch, where the fuck are you?"

My cell phone rang, and I anxiously looked at the screen hoping it was Dutch. The number was Restricted.

"Hello," I answered hoping to hear his voice on the other end.

"Yo', what's up ma. This Xa right?" The voice was not familiar to me, but it was a dude.

"Uh, who the fuck is this?"

"Dutch told me to hit you. He locked up."

He was locked up? Oh shit.

"Now, you gotta listen very carefully. D wants you to go on his laptop and get the combination to his safe. It's saved in a file called Double D. The password on his laptop is deluxe99. He wants you to take everything out of the safe in the back of the master bedroom's closet. It's one briefcase and a large black bag. There'll also be a flash drive in there. Destroy that shit. Fire will be sufficient. Don't open none of the bags 'till you get home. You understand?"

"Yes..."

"There's more. 'Cause of what will be in your possession you can't fly, ride the train, or the bus. You'll have to be driven. D's driver Henry will pick you up in about thirty minutes. That's all the time you have before you gotta be outta there. The police will be there in about an hour with a search warrant. You'll have two separate drivers. One will drive you from here to South Carolina. The next will take you to Miami. Everything is mapped out. I will call you back with more instructions in forty five minutes."

I was literally shaking when I hung up the phone. Damn, the police were on the way and if they found whatever was in that safe, I'd probably get locked up too. Getting myself together, I grabbed the laptop, put the password in and found the file on the desktop with the safe's code. After getting the items, I grabbed my shit and rushed outside.

The white Benz pulled up and Henry was driving. Boy was I relieved to see him. We hurriedly got everything inside and rolled out. I had a feeling I knew what was in the huge, black bag, but I didn't say shit. I don't know why I didn't just say fuck that and left, but I just felt something pulling me into going along with it.

Henry gave me a comforting smile, but didn't say much as he drove. I didn't feel there was anything to talk about either. Then the mystery man called me back.

"Once you get to South Carolina, Henry's gonna drop you off at a Courtyard Marriot. You gon' chill and try to get some rest. Check out at ten. Another driver in a black BMW will be waiting for you."

Umm, didn't they think those flashy ass calls would call attention to us?

"There's an ID in the back in the car for you to use. You're a rich heiress, so the police won't bother you."

Well, that explained that.

"Okay..." I simply muttered waiting for him to say something else.

Not knowing if I should trust the dude on the other line, or Henry, I didn't know what else to do. One thing I did know was not to ask too many questions.

"A'ight, you'll hear from me again soon." The mystery man hung up.

A few hours later Henry asked me if I was hungry. He said Celesto had prepared something for us to eat. We didn't really have time to stop unless I had to pee. I killed the fried chicken, red beans and yellow rice. After that I fell asleep.

The drive was long as hell, but we made it to our destination after a few stops. The entire time, my mind was on Dutch. Henry gave me a bag of weed.

"Hopefully that will help. Take care Miss Xa." He also handed me a stack of hundred-dollar bills.

After that I checked into my room under the assumed name not sure what would happen next. With the bags safely under the bed, I secured the door and tried not to be too damn jittery. The entire time I wasn't able to sleep. It didn't matter how much I smoked, or how many pills I popped.

The next day I met my last driver, Ivan. Once I was in the car, my phone rang.

"When you get to Miami I will call and tell you where to meet me," the familiar voice instructed.

My curiosity was killing me, and I was also hoping Dutch would somehow be able to call. After sleeping most of the time, because I tossed and turned the night before, I was finally home. Damn, I was relieved as hell. With Ivan's help, I got everything inside.

Once he left, my phone rang. It was the mystery caller.

"You can open the bags now to see what's inside. I know you gon' have a lot of questions. I'll text you the address I want you to meet me at. Be here in an hour."

Nervously, I unzipped the duffel bag first. It was full of bricks of cocaine.

"Shit," I exhaled. Although I figured it was drugs, it just occurred to me that I'd trafficked at least twenty kilos across state lines.

The briefcase was full of hundreds. There had to be at least a million dollars in there.

At that point, I still didn't have a car, so I asked Sita to use hers.

"Hurry up. I gotta be somewhere in a few hours."

"Okay," I told her as I grabbed her keys from the key holder by the front door.

In less than forty-five minutes, I pulled up to a condo complex. It was nice as hell. In no time I found the number of his condo and used the brass knocker.

The door swung open and I was face to face with a fine ass almond tone skinned dude, with big brown eyes, a zaddy beard, and nice muscles.

"Sup Xa, I'm Ramon." He introduced himself and invited me in.

"Well, what's this all about?" I asked Ramon as I placed the bags on the sofa. "I'on know shit 'bout how to sell no dope."

"Well, that's where I come in. I do business wit' Dutch. He needs that money for his lawyer though. You gon' take it to him. That nigga's facing fifteen years and, so he gotta pay big. Umm, he wants you to take twenty-five stacks for yourself for your troubles. It's five hundred stacks in all."

And I thought it was a million. Well, I was close.

"The rest goes to his lawyer. As far as that, I'll give you all the info you need. When it comes to the keys, I'm gon' help you flip them. In the process I'll teach you everything you need to know 'bout the game. Dutch wants to make sure you good and he didn't want that shit in the spot when the po po busted in."

"What you gettin' out of this?"

He licked his lips and lit a blunt that was behind his ear. As he took a pull, he seemed to be thinking about how to answer that question.

"That nigga was right when he said you was fine, so lookin' at you is enough. However, I'm due half of the cut from them keys."

"What if I don't wanna have anything to do wit' this shit."

Shrugging his shoulders nonchalantly, he said, "Well, that shit's up to you. You can leave it all here now and I'll get a bitch who need that twenty-five K to take the money to the lawyer. Then I'll flip them birds myself. Free profit."

"Shit, fuck it, I'm in."

That was how I descended into the underbelly of the illegal drug trade and damn a bitch was stacking. In less than two months I quit my job at Shadows, bought a brand-new Range and got my own spot. The more I hustled, the more I got addicted to that shit. At that point, I'd do any and everything for that paper and I gave zero fucks about it.

Chapter 15

Atlanta

2017

It was my last night in Atlanta and I wanted to turn the fuck up before I left. Alicia had invited me to a house party one of Jermaine's homeboys were having. I ended up riding with her there, because I didn't feel like driving. Besides, I planned to get pissy drunk.

When we got there the yard was packed, with cars. Those shits were bumper to bumper, and I hoped we didn't get blocked in when we wanted to leave. The music was loud as fuck and I wondered if the neighbors would complain about that shit. At that point, I didn't care. I just wanted to party.

Whoever was throwing the party had pushed the furniture against the wall to make a dance floor. There was a makeshift bar set up and food was galore. They even had a real damn DJ in there spinning.

"This shit is lit," I told Alicia.

Jermaine was with us of course, but that was cool. He was just one of those insecure ass men who couldn't trust his woman out and about without him. I decided that was Alicia's problem, not mine.

"Hell yeah, let's go get a drink." She grabbed my hand and led me away as Jermaine greeted a bunch of dudes.

After pouring some Hennessey and Coke, I decided to mingle. Shit, it was nothing wrong with getting my flirt on. I'd be gone soon anyway. A one night stand even crossed my mind, because it was some fine niggas up in that bitch. Damn!

Once I had a few drinks in my system I was loose and ready to dance. I joined the crowd on the floor and showed them bitches how to twerk. All eyes were on me and soon, I got the attention of some fine ass chocolate nigga. He smelled good as hell as he held on to me.

"Damn shawty," he said breathlessly as I took it to a whole different level.

Tired of dancing, I was ready to smoke something. Walking away from dude, I found Alicia and sparked up a blunt I'd rolled up earlier. We got blazed and were talking when dude who was dancing with me approached. I knew he'd be on it.

"You know gettin' away from me wasn't going to be that damn easy. What's yo' name?"

"Xa," I told him. "What's yours?"

"Ryan, but you can call me Ry."

"Cool, nice to meet you Ry."

"So, where yo' fine ass from?" He licked his lips and sipped his Heineken.

"I'm originally from here, but I live in Miami."

"Word, that's what's up. I'm tryna get yo' number so I can call you. I wanna get to know…"

Before he could finish that mufucka Eddie stood between us.

"This me man," he told dude as he grabbed my arm and led me away.

"What the fuck you doin'?" Yanking away from him I rolled my eyes in annoyance.

"Gettin' you away from that lame, crab ass nigga. What you doin' yo'? Accordin' to you, you got enough niggas in Miami. Why you tryna add to the list? Let me find out you turned into..."

"My mama?" I asked him as I shook my head. "It don't even matter Eddie. I'm grown as fuck and you ain't my nigga. What I do with my pussy is my fuckin' business, so get the fuck on wit that shit. Like I told you before, I don't need you to protect me."

Sauntering off, I sat down on the sofa to get my thoughts together. Why did he insist on acting like were still together? My ass was so damn high, it felt like the room was spinning. What the hell was in that weed? I had got that shit from Ramon before I left. Eddie just stared at me and I looked away. When my eyes landed on the door, I saw a familiar face walk in. That bitch Chloe had the nerve to show up.

She looked around and then headed in my direction with a stank ass look on her face. Sobering up immediately, I was ready for whatever. Stopping in front of me, she put her hands on her hips.

"Can you please finally listen to me?" The bitch had the nerve to ask with an attitude.

Staring at her blankly, I didn't even answer the hoe. If anything, I was trying my best not to act on my ongoing anger. That shit hadn't gone anywhere. How the fuck was that hoe going to ask me if I was going to finally listen to her dumb ass like I owed her something?

"Eddie came on to me and although I know I was wrong, I'm human. You still mad at me 'bout that shit, but I been moved on. I'm sure you have too. I mean, back then I was on some selfish shit, but y'en even give me the chance to apologize. I know I hurt you, but Eddie told me you wasn't fuckin' him right and..."

Her words were knocked right out of her when my fist landed right in that bitch's face. She was stunned as if she didn't know what hit her ass. Dragging her across the floor by her hair, I swung her around like a rag dog. Everybody was hyping up the fight as I kicked and stumped that hoe.

"Fuck you bitch! You should've just stayed the fuck away from me! I'on wanna hear that bullshit!"

Shit, the way I saw it, it didn't matter if I was fucking that nigga good or not. As my friend it wasn't her place to do it right. She should've left that up to another hoe. Reaching down, I wrapped my fingers around that bitch's neck and squeezed with everything in me. The desire to watch her pathetic ass life slip away was so strong that I started to squeeze even tighter. Her eyes were blood shot red and her skin was the color of a tomato.

Suddenly, I felt myself being pulled away from Chloe. Somebody else was attempting to pry my fingers from her neck, but I was squeezing so hard, it was nearly impossible.

"Let her go Xa!" I heard Alicia yelling at me, but she sounded like she was far away.

Then I heard Eddie's voice. "C'mon baby, you gon' kill her man. Let her go! It ain't worth it Xa. Let her go."

Finally coming to my senses, I released that hoe and allowed Eddie and Alicia to break us up. With a satisfied smirk, I laughed at the bald spot in the front of that bitch's head. A large clump of her hair was on the floor. Chloe coughed and tried to catch her breath. As she looked at me she shook her head.

"Bitch! You done lost yo' fuckin' mind!" Tears fell down her cheeks. "You could've killed me."

"Believe me, I wanted to, so bad. Eddie was right though. It ain't worth it. You gon' suffer for what you did bitch. It's just a matter of fuckin' time! I promise you that!" After spitting in her swollen face, I looked at Alicia. "I'm ready to go."

"I'll take you home," Eddie volunteered way too quickly.

Rolling my eyes, I got ready to protest, but Alicia spoke up. "Yeah, 'cause ma already callin' complainin' 'bout how my baby won't go to sleep. I can go pick my girls up."

Rolling my eyes, I walked off feeling angry enough to beat Eddie down too.

"Xa," she called out behind me. "Make sure you come see me before you leave."

"A'ight. I'm pullin' out early though," I threw over my shoulder watching as Chloe left with her face all bloody and shit.

I'd rocked that bitch.

"You know I'm always up by six."

With a nod, I left wishing she'd helped me decline the ride with her brother.

* * *

The car ride started out quiet as hell, but of course, Eddie broke the silence. "Nothing I can do or say will change what I did to you. Me and Chloe were wrong as fuck. I ain't gon' keep apologizin' 'cause the fact that I never touched her again should tell you I regretted it. She lied yo'. I heard what she told you. That bitch popped up at the crib crying and shit about how much she loved me and wanted to be with me. It ain't no excuse for it, but I fell for the bullshit. She told me you was cheatin' on me and that's why you wasn't fuckin' me like that. The only reason I believed her was 'cause she was yo' girl and I thought she'd know. Once you walked in on us, I knew the bitch was lyin' 'cause when it came down to it, she ran out that bitch. If she was tellin' the truth, she would've stood up to you 'bout that shit. It was too late to fix it by then. I should have talked to you, but I was bein' a selfish mufucka. That was immature as hell of me. I'm older now though, Xa. I may not have recognized what I had then, but I do now. Although it's probably too damn late, I can't help but still love you. I'm still in love wit' you and I still wanna marry you. It's never been a moment when I stopped wanting that, never."

"Not even when you was fuckin' Chloe? You even wanted to marry me when you was dickin' down my friend?" Rolling my eyes, I still wasn't down for the bullshit.

Eddie glanced over at me and said with a straight face, "Yeah, I even wanted to marry you when I was dickin' down yo' friend. I can face up to my shit. Don't you think it's time to let that go? I'm a man now and I ain't that boy you was wit' five years ago. I can make you happy again. You know I did before. Now I got my own shit and we can have that life together we always wanted."

"You don't know me anymore Eddie. The young girl who wanted a life with you is gone. I'm a totally different person and you probably won't feel the same once you get to know who I am now."

"I'll love you no matter what Xa. That's my good word."

His phone rang, and he looked down at the screen with a line of wrinkles in his forehead.

"Sup man?" He answered.

There was a long pause and Eddie shook his

head in frustration. "Fuck, not again. Okay, I'm on my way now."

"Umm, on your way where? I hope you droppin' me off first."

"My crib is on the way to your mama's. My pit bull Killer got out of the fence somehow and is roamin' the damn neighborhood. That was my neighbor. I gotta make sure I secure his crazy ass 'fore he kill some damn body."

Not saying a word, I was pissed the fuck off. I should've drove myself to that damn party because now I had to be around that nigga longer than I wanted to be. Then I glanced over at him and thought about it. He was smelling so damn tasty and I had to admit that Eddie was finer than ever. He'd always been good looking, but with age came a lot more muscle and swag. Damn, his dick was probably even better. I had to press my thighs together.

"So, you cool?" He asked.

Shrugging, I said, "I guess I have no choice."

"I ain't gon' lie. I was kinda glad to see you dust that bitch for lyin' and shit."

"I ain't fight that bitch 'cause of you. I fought her because I needed to let some pent-up aggression out of me."

"You just need some good dick," he chuckled.

"Dick is never a need for me nigga. It's always a want," I checked him. "I can get dick all day every fuckin' day."

"I'm sure you can. You can definitely get mine."

"Who can't? I'on feel special." Cracking a smile, I let him know that I was fucking with him.

He laughed. "That's fucked up."

"I mean, the truth is the truth. I'on know 'bout now, but you had that community dick back then."

"Yeah, I was a hoe, but I done learned the hard way shawty. It ain't about how many bitches I can fuck no more. I'd rather have that one special lady in my life. I miss you Xa. Straight up, shawty. I miss the fuck out of you man. I ain't tryna make this 'bout me, 'cause I know you were the one who was hurt in the situation. It was all my fault, but you the only woman I ever sat up nights and cried over."

That made me feel something shift for Eddie, although I'd been the one crying over him for so many nights. Maybe whooping Chloe's ass was just therapeutic. He deserved an ass whooping just as much as she did though. Maybe I'd just get some of that dick and go back to Florida on his ass. There was no way I could ever be in a relationship with Eddie again, but I didn't see anything wrong with fucking him one last time.

* * *

The night was still young, so after Eddie secured his dog, he invited me in for a drink.

"I promise, I'll take you back to your mom's after. It's just... I know you leavin' tomorrow and I wanna spend a little more time wit' you."

"Why you wanna spend time wit' me when all I've been doin' is bitchin' at you?"

That was something I didn't understand. From the moment I saw him at the gas station, I'd been giving that nigga the cold shoulder and some choice words.

He grinned, and my iced-out heart stopped.

"Mmm, I love a challenge."

Shaking my head, I had to laugh at that. Maybe that was our issue. I wasn't a challenge for Eddie. Being that I was so in love with him, I was always accessible. We were like a married couple when I was only sixteen. Damn, did he cheat on me because I didn't keep him on his toes?

"Look Eddie, I'm gon' take you up on that drink, but I ain't tryna be a challenge. Don't get too damn drunk, 'cause you takin' me back to my mom's."

"A'ight, I gotcha," he agreed and opened my car door.

His house was really gorgeous, and he lived in a nice ass neighborhood. As I looked around the foyer, I couldn't help but fantasize about how our life would've been. The sound of little feet running around and cook outs in the back yard all came to mind. We'd probably have at least one child by now. Shaking my head, I returned to reality just as he said my name.

"Xa, c'mon, let's go to the kitchen."

All the state of the art stainless steel appliances and gadgets you could think of were in his large kitchen. I fell in love with the space immediately. My place was nicely decorated but my kitchen was meh. When I sat down at the bar, he asked me what I wanted to drink. I decided to stick with Hennessey since that was what I was drinking at the party.

We grabbed our drinks and he led me to the kitchen table before pulling out the dominoes. We used to play strip dominoes all the time and he'd always win.

"I ain't played bones in years." A smile spread on my face as I recalled fond memories.

"We ain't gotta strip if you don't wanna." There was a sly smile on his face.

"Nah, you like a challenge, and so do I, so let's do it."

My smile was just as sly as his by that time.

After about thirty minutes of playing that nigga was down to his boxers and wife beater. I had only taken off my shoes.

"You must've forgot how to play or you just tryna show me the D," I teased.

"You wanna see the D?"

"I've seen it before."

Letting out a chuckle, he put the bones on the table and stood up. Then he walked over to the wall where a speaker was mounted. He turned it on and the sound of some old R&B filled my ears.

Was that Avant's "When We Make Sweet Love?"
Uh ohh, here we go. We'd been reminiscing, and I
was acting civil, so I guess he thought that was his
cue to make his move.

Standing in front of me, he had a serious
ass look on his face. He dropped down to his knees.
Taking my hand into his, he raised it to his lips for a
kiss. Staring up at me, it was as if he was ready to
propose again.

"You are even more beautiful now than
ever Xa. I gotta admit, I been hoping for the day I'd
see your beautiful face again. Although we ain't
together, it's good to know that I didn't lose you
forever. It's like… a fantasy right now, to have you
in my presence again. Damn, my head's so gone
over you. It's like… I can't love nobody because you
took my heart wit' you when you left."

Tears glistened in his eyes and I had to look
away. That nigga was getting too deep for me.
What he didn't know was, I could never love
because I'd left my heart there with him. I'd never
thought of it that way and it made me want to
reevaluate everything I'd thought up until that
moment. It wasn't easy for me to change my views
now that life had hardened me. To keep my sanity,
I couldn't allow him to break down that wall I'd
built.

As he stood, I began to talk. "Eddie, I…"
But before I could finish his lips were on
mine and his tongue was parting them. When his
tongue invaded the space it hadn't been in in

years, I didn't bother to fight it. Instead, I got lost in it. By far, he was the best kisser out of any man I'd ever kissed in my life. The way he was sucking on my tongue had me wetter than any ocean.

"Mmm..." He pulled away and stared into my eyes. "It's something else I've been dyin' to taste."

The look he was giving me was intense enough to make my panties fall the fuck off. As he reached down to remove my jeans, I didn't object. I just stepped out of them. Now, you may be questioning my logic? Why did I beat Chloe's ass and was about to give Eddie some ass? Some things just didn't have be explained. See, I was now a woman who could separate love and sex. My horny ass wanted to cum. Nothing more, nothing less.

After he removed my panties, he buried his face between my legs and inhaled. The look on his face was of pure ecstasy. As he stared up at me in longing, he gestured for me to sit back down in the kitchen chair. Once I was seated, he lifted my foot and started sucking on my big toe. Then he took all my toes into his mouth and sucked them.

"Ohhh... Eddie... mmm..." That shit felt good as hell.

Then he did the same to my other foot before making a hot trail up to my thigh with his tongue. Spreading my thighs with his strong hands he held them wide open as he feasted on my pussy. He'd suck my clit and then slide his tongue inside of me simultaneously. In no time, I was weak and trying desperately to get away from his sweet tongue's assault.

"Mmm... you like fine wine shawty. You taste better wit' time..." His eyes were on me as I watched his tongue swirl and twirl expertly around my clit.

"You've gotten better wit' time." Something told me that practice made perfect.

He'd always been good at eating pussy, but I didn't have any other experience back then to know that for sure. I could tell that he'd perfected his craft over time now that I had something to prepare his skills to.

"Ohhh..." My leg was starting to shake, and he flashed a mischievous smile at me.

He knew that he had the best of me, but I'd get that ass back. My eyes bore into his and we stared each other down as if it was a duel. I was losing like a mufucka.

"Uhh... mmm... Eddie..."

Not having to tell him I was cuming, I knew he could tell. He found that spot that he knew would take me there and concentrated on sucking on it. That was it. A bitch was tapping out and damn if I wasn't loving it.

Eddie picked me up and carried me over to the kitchen counter. That nigga thought he was going up in me raw, but I had some news for his ass.

"Umm, you better wrap that shit up if you want some of this." I covered my pussy up with my hands and everything.

"Shit, I tried." He shrugged his shoulders. "Don't move."

Watching as he walked off, I couldn't help but admire his muscular ass. He was back in less than a minute and he looked up at me to see if I was having second thoughts. I wasn't. After that I damn sure did want some of that dick. Shit, I almost wanted to suck it, but nah. Fuck that.

When he pulled it out, my mouth did water. I could remember a time when I'd wake his ass up to some hella head. Those days were over though and although he'd taught me how to suck a mean dick, he wasn't going to get a sample of what I could do now. My skills had evolved, and he wasn't ready. I didn't need him acting more in love than he already was.

After he slid the condom on, he grabbed my ass and took me on an orgasmic ride. I mean, I was slobbering because that shit was so good.

"Look at me," he demanded every single time I tried to close my eyes or look away.

That nigga even cupped my chin in his hand and said, "I want you to see who makin' you cum like that."

"Damn Eddie..." I whimpered when I couldn't take any more of the way he was giving me that deep stroke grind from the back.

He gave me some mercy and relieved me of about an inch. Then he went back in. He picked me up and carried me to his bedroom while he was still inside of me. That was when the roles reversed, and I rode him backwards like a cowgirl.

As I leaned over, grabbed his ankles and twerked on that dick for dear life, it was over for us both.

"Arggghhhh... fuck!" His fingers dug into the flesh of my ass and I knew he'd left prints there.

"Mmm... Eddie... yessss..."

Riding that shit out, I waited for the tingles to subside to lift myself up from him. Then I remembered that he was wearing a condom and I hoped it didn't break. Shit, I was riding the hell out of that nigga.

After we both washed off, we chilled together in his bed. It was after three am, and I was getting tired.

"You gon' take me home or nah?"

"Nah."

Frowning at him, I said, "But you told me you'd take me home."

"That was before you gave me some pussy. Now I want you to stay wit' me."

Rolling my eyes, I had to clarify something for him. "We just fucked Eddie. That's it. It don't mean I wanna lay up wit' you tonight."

"Don't downplay what just happened. You was feelin' it. I know because I was inside you. I could feel it too."

"Okay, it was good, but don't expect nothing."

"Why not? I still fuckin' love you. That wasn't just sex to me."

"Eddie, what do you want from me?"

"I want you back. I want what we had."

"That's over. I have a home and a life in Florida."

"And you could have a home and a life here wit' me. What's so important in Florida that you gotta run back to?"

Honestly, there wasn't any way for me to answer that question to make him understand.

"I can't Eddie..."

"You can, but you keep holdin' on to the past." He put his arms around me and kissed the back of my neck. "You just need some time and as long as you promise not to count me out, I'll wait. Just spend the night wit' me. I just wanna hold you in my arms again."

Giving in, I laid down and let him wrap his arms around me. Holding me in the spooning position, he nuzzled his face in my neck. In no time at all he was asleep, but my mind was reeling, and it took me a long time to doze off.

Chapter 16

Atlanta

2017

When I woke up, that shit was like déjà vu. A mufucka in a black ski mask was standing over me with a handgun pointed in my face. My heart immediately dropped. When I looked, there was another dude in a black ski mask standing over Eddie with an AK pointed at him.

"Rise and shine, bitch ass nigga!" The one with his gun on Eddie yelled and let out a menacing laugh.

"The fuck...?" Eddie asked as he jumped up

"Shut the fuck up nigga, you know what it is," the one with his gun on me said. "You care 'bout this bitch?" He asked Eddie.

"Hell yeah. Don't hurt her. Just tell me what the fuck you want."

"I want yo' stash nigga. The drugs and the money, but I know it ain't here. You gon' take me to it, while my nigga stay here wit' yo' bitch. If you give a fuck about her, you won't play no games. You got me, nigga? If you fuck around and do some dumb shit that bitch's dead!" Spit flew and hit me right smack dab on the lip.

Instinctively, I frowned up my face and wanted to wipe my mouth, but I couldn't. The gunmen's threats were real as fuck along with their weapons. I played it cool, stayed still and kept my mouth shut.

"Get up and get dressed nigga. We 'bout to take a ride. Nigga, tie that bitch up and shit 'till we get back. I'on need her tryna sneak off and call the damn cops."

His partner nodded and pulled me up from the bed. He led me downstairs with the gun to my head. After tying me up to the kitchen table with rope, he covered my mouth with duct tape. A few minutes later the other gunman marched down the stairs with Eddie in tow.

"I'm so sorry baby," Eddie told me as the dude pushed him toward the front door.

Tears filled my eyes as he gave me the most vulnerable look I'd ever seen in my life. It wasn't that he was scared, but he was more afraid for my safety. One thing I knew about Eddie was he was no punk and he'd do anything in his power to keep me alive.

The masked intruder didn't say anything to me as we waited. Instead he paced the floor like he was nervous as hell. If I could get lose, I'd probably have a good chance of getting out of the situation because his head didn't seem to be in it.

As my eyes followed him, I started to wonder what was going on with Eddie? Was he complying with dude, or would he defy him and try to kill him? The Eddie that I knew wouldn't go out without a fight, but threatening my life might've changed that.

Over an hour had passed by before Eddie and the other dude got back. Damn, I was relieved as fuck.

"A'ight nigga, let's get outta here," the gunman told the one who was watching over me. "He can untie that bitch."

Eddie was just standing there, but as soon as the gunmen turned their backs to leave, the sound of a single gunshot rang out.

Pop!

When I looked to my left, I saw that Eddie had retrieved a gun that must've been stashed in a drawer. One of the gunmen laid bleeding on the floor as the other fled.

Pop! Pop! Pop!

Eddie went after him and kept on shooting as he did. The second gunman ran to the car as he ducked and dodged the bullets. He shot back as he got behind the wheel.

Pow! Pow!

Eddie moved behind the door for cover and when he realized that the other dude had got away, he started cursing.

"Fuck! He got away wit' my shit!"

My eyes casted down to the man who was bleeding to death on the floor. Eddie walked over to untie me and removed the duct tape from my mouth.

"You okay babe?" He hugged me as I wept frantically.

"Yes... are you?"

"Shit, I'm alive, but that nigga got away wit' the money I been savin' up for years. My plan was to get outta the game by next year. He got away with 'bout ten keys too. Fuck! Now I gotta start the fuck over."

He got up and walked over to that nigga who was bleeding out. After he kicked him in the groin, he leaned over to remove his mask. My eyes were glued to his face.

"You know him?" I asked Eddie. Maybe he had plenty of enemies in the streets. Obviously, his status and reputation had grown in the along with his stash.

"Nah, I'on know this fuck nigga. I gotta clean this shit up and get rid of this mufucka. Let me get you home. I'm sorry shit happened like this."

"I guess it was too good to be true that we were gettin' along." Wiping the tears from my eyes, I was glad as hell to get out of there.

"I know right. He ain't do shit to you, did he?"

"No," I shook my head. "To be honest, if I wasn't tied up, I'm sure I could've took his ass myself. He seemed like he wasn't really... used to doin' shit like this."

"I'm just glad you good."

He pulled me into him for a bear hug.

"I'm shaken up, but I'm okay. I just uh, I'm ready to go."

After I grabbed my purse, I walked outside and popped a Xan with no water. My nerves were shot, but I tried to hold it together. Eddie joined me on the porch and then walked me to his car.

"I'm sure you ready to leave now and go back to Florida. I'm sorry man. I know I'm a target, but..."

"I'm more worried 'bout you Eddie. I mean, you said you'd been savin' that money for years. Was that your whole stash?"

"Yup. One and a half million dollars." He shook his head.

"Damn. At least you're alive though, I mean, that's a lot to lose, don't get me wrong, but you can always try and make that shit back. Your life is another story. Once that's gone, that's gone."

"Shit, I guess, but damn. I been savin' for five fuckin' years. You know, I started savin' that shit for us, but..."

"Wow, we'd be livin' it up by now then. One and a half million is a lot."

"Two was the goal, but they took my dope, so..." He hit the steering wheel over and over. "Fuck!"

Trying to calm him down, I put my hand on his knee and rubbed. "It could've been much worse Eddie."

"Shit, you right, but I'm pissed. I wanna get that other nigga, but I'on know where to start lookin' for his ass."

"Well, at least you got one of 'em."

He looked over at me. "Nah, no matter what, at least I had the chance to have you in my bed again. That's all that matters. I know you gon' got back to Florida, but I just want you to keep in touch wit' me. I don't wanna lose you... again."

Not knowing what to say, being that it was a dedicate moment, I didn't want to seem like an asshole. "We'll see what happens Eddie."

"That's all I can ask for," he said softly.

The truth was, I didn't know if I wanted to keep in touch with Eddie after that. My life had been filled with strife and one fucked up thing after another. I'd been forever changed and there was no going back Even if I wanted to be with Eddie, my malevolent side wouldn't allow me to do it. It was just almost impossible for me to give a fuck anymore. No matter how much I loved him in the past, love just wasn't for me now. I'd gotten what I wanted from him and I'd enjoyed the fuck out of it. Well, except for having a gun in my face.

Eddie pulled up in front of my mother's house and leaned over to kiss me. That time, I cut the kiss short and he looked disappointed as hell.

"Uh, I guess that shit that happened changed everything huh?" His eyes searched mine.

"You're a man Eddie. You already know how shit works. Yeah, what just happened was fucked up, but even if that didn't happen, I don't know if anything would've came of last night. It just... happened. We both got caught up in the moment and..."

"No, hell no. It was more than that. It felt like way more than that to me."

Shaking my head, I opened the car door and stepped out. "No, it wasn't. It was just a nut. I'm glad you're okay Eddie, but I have to go."

As I got out of the car and closed the door, I felt his eyes glued to me. Damn, if only he'd get over it. Yeah, the dick was awesome, and the head was even better, but there was nothing there. Even after all the sweet talk and Shakespearean moments, I realized that I was over it. Not even a life, or death situation made me want to be with him. Eddie was just a part of my past and it was time to let it all go once and for all.

"Xa!" He yelled out as I made my way up the steps to my mother's door.

"What Eddie?" I asked as I turned around.

"If I could go back in time, I'd change everything. You know that."

With a nod, I had to admit, "Me too."

Tears burned my eyes, but I willed them away. It was time to move on for real. I'd been holding on to old feelings and harboring emotions that I'd kept bottled in from the past. Would I ever be able to feel like none of that mattered anymore? I felt like I could, but only time would tell for sure.

After I had everything packed up in my car, I hugged my mother.

"Thank you for giving me a second chance baby girl. I love you so much. To be honest, you're the only thing I've ever done right in my life."

"I love you too ma."

"When are you comin' back?"

"Hopefully it'll be for you wedding." I smiled and leaned back against my Range.

"Well, you never know what the future holds. Shoot, I ain't think you'd ever talk to me again, but look at how God works."

With a smile, I opened my car door. "You are right about that ma."

I got behind the wheel and started the ignition. She waved at me as I drove off and headed to Alicia's. One thing I couldn't do was leave without seeing her.

* * *

It was a little after eight in the morning and like Alicia had said, she was up. The girls were sitting at the table eating pancakes and eggs and Jermaine was at work.

"You want some breakfast?" Alicia asked.

"No, I don't really have an appetite after..."

"Yeah, Eddie told me about that shi..."

She caught herself and led me out of the kitchen. "They pick everything up like a sponge, especially the bad words. I have to watch what I say."

"I feel you girl. We had some foul mouths listenin' to our mamas."

"Speaking of mamas. Ma's here."

Margie came from around the corner and without saying a word, pulled me into a tight hug. It was so good to see her, and I couldn't contain my tears.

"You thought you was gon' leave without seein' me?" She asked. "I'm just glad you and Eddie are okay. People are so crazy."

"I'm glad too and you're right. People are crazy." I agreed trying not to get too mushy.

No matter how much I had been hurt by men in the past, Margie had always been my saving grace. Never had she judged or shunned me like everybody else. I could honestly say that Margie and Alicia were two of the few people who had always been there for me. Their loyalty proved that there were people capable of giving a fuck. The sad part was, after what I'd been through, I didn't know if I could be one of them.

We talked for a few minutes and then she rushed off to check up on the girls. Alicia glanced over at me.

"Why are you goin' back to Florida?"

"I live there Alicia."

"Well, just like you moved there you can move back here."

"It's not that easy now."

"Why?" She glared at me. "It was that easy then. You had real, ever lasting friendships that spanned longer than five years here and it was easy for you to leave. Why is it so damn hard for you to stay?"

"Honestly Alicia, I love you and Margie, but it's just too hard for me to be here. There're too many fucked up memories."

"But there are good ones too. The good ones outweigh the bad."

"Well, the bad was so bad that it seems to outweigh the good to me. I'm sorry, but I gotta go Licia."

Her phone started ringing. "Hold up a second."

She looked at the screen and her eyes widened. "It's Chloe."

Rolling my eyes, I waited for her to answer that bitch's call. For some reason, Alicia put her on speakerphone. I hoped she wasn't still trying to play mediator. If so, she'd already failed miserably at that shit.

"What's up Chloe? It's early as fuck."

"Bitch, that's 'cause I got a call from the fuckin' ob/gyn last week to come in for my test results today. It's fucked up that I had to show up wit' my face all messed up and shit, but you won't believe this."

"What?" Alicia asked.

"Remember that nigga I was telling you about that I met on Plenty of Fish that's from VA?"

"Yeah, what about him?"

"Well, I ain't tell you this, but we met up in South Carolina 'bout a fuckin' month ago. We'd been talkin' on the phone and video chatting for at least two months before I agreed to meet his ass.

Of course, when we met up, we fucked. That shit was good as fuck, we kicked it and then I came home. After that, this nigga deleted his profile off Plenty of Fish and Facebook. His phone is disconnected and all. I'm like, what the fuck? So, this nigga just disappeared into thin fuckin' air. I can't find him on Instagram, Twitter or nothing. So, now it's time for my check up and shit and I tested positive for fuckin' herpes bitch! Fuckin' herpes! He's the only nigga I fucked..."

"Chloe, don't tell me you met some nigga online and fucked him without a fuckin' condom. Please don't."

"No bitch. Check this shit the fuck out. We spent the whole weekend at Myrtle Beach. He left before me, 'cause my ass was wore out from all that fuckin'. Before I left the room, I found what looked like part of a condom on the floor. That made me think that nigga broke the damn condom on purpose. So, I call him to confront his ass and he didn't fuckin' answer. I'm like damn, what the fuck? Now I see that nigga's a dirty dick fuck boy!" She busted into tears and I didn't feel any ounce of sorry for the hoe.

Rolling my eyes, I hoped it was a sign that I couldn't care less.

"That's fucked up Chloe, damn. What you gon' do?"

"I'on know bitch. I can't find that nigga. Shit, it's bad enough that I got into that shit with Xa, and the next day I find out some shit like this. I was hopin' that bump on my pussy was nothing. Fuck! I wish I'd never met that nigga!" The bitch started wailing and I started laughing.

"Who the fuck is that?" Chloe asked. "You got me on speaker bitch?"

Alicia hurried up and took her off speaker phone. "That's the TV. Hell, nah bitch. What the fuck? Look, I'm gon' call you right back. Let me get the girls cleaned up. Okay."

She ended the call and looked at me. "Why did you do that? That shit ain't funny."

"Not to you, but it damn sure is to me." Not able to contain myself, I couldn't help but laugh again. I laughed even harder, I had to slap myself on the knee. "Whew, that bumpy pussy bitch is distraught. Yasss!"

"You wrong as hell Xa."

"I don't give a shit. She was wrong and karma's a big bitch. Now, let me get outta here."

"You really gon' leave today after what my brother went through? I mean, y'all did spend the night together, so I assume you fucked. Some nigga took all his money and he had to kill the other? Do you give a fuck?

"Do I give a fuck? I had a gun in my face too. It's nothing I can do to change that shit. I have to go on with my life. I'm a grown woman and I can fuck my ex if I want to and go back home. What can I do now, Alicia, huh? It ain't like I can get his money back. What Eddie does is dangerous, and I'on want no part of his lifestyle."

She shook her head. "Well, I think you're bein' selfish."

"You can feel however you want. My life isn't here anymore. Bye Alicia."

* * *

About thirty minutes later, I pulled up to a Doubletree Hotel in Marietta. After making a call, I waited for an answer.

"Sup shawty?"

"I'm outside."

"A'ight."

That nigga came out loaded down with at least three bags. He put them in the trunk, opened the door and got in the passenger seat. Then he leaned over to kiss me.

"You okay?" His eyes scanned over me as if he was making sure.

"Yeah, but it's too bad yo' boy got killed and shit."

"That's why I wanna go back and finish that nigga the fuck off!" His eyes filled with anger.

"Ramon, let's be realistic. You don't think that nigga's gon' be prepared for you to come back? Shit, we got a million and a half dollars that we don't have to split three ways now. Think about it."

With that said, he seemed to calm down a little bit.

"You right, but where's the fuckin' money." I wanted to see that shit.

"I put it in the trunk."

243 | A Heartless Goon Snatched My Soul

"Well, I wanna see it."

That nigga sighed and got out of the car. I popped the trunk and he got back in with the bag. He unzipped it and I saw the stacks of hundred-dollar bills. The way that shit smelled made me rub my hands together greedily.

"The keys back there too, right?" The hustler in me was ready to get to Miami so I could put that stolen product on the streets. Like Ramon said about that shit that Dutch had given me, it was free profit.

"Yeah babe. We good. Shit, wit' this lick, we gon' be runnin' Miami. For real. Fuck that, we gon' run the whole east coast."

With a smile on my face, I headed toward the freeway. There was a long ass drive ahead, but it was going to all be worth it. The way I saw it, I finally had what Eddie owed me. See, love was just a second-hand emotion. That shit had got me nowhere but hurt. Fuck love. That shit was overrated anyway. Money was much better.

We stopped to get something quick to eat and we both used the bathroom before heading out. The trip from Atlanta to Miami would take about nine hours. Almost eight hours had passed by and that nigga Ramon was knocked out. He was snoring, slobbering and all. When I pulled over on the side of the road, that nigga woke up. Looking over at me, he rubbed his eyes, and asked groggily, "What the fuck you stoppin' for."

I put my nine-millimeter to his temple, glad

that his window was down so I wouldn't make a mess. "I ain't lettin' a snake ass nigga like you have my fuckin' money."

It was a good thing Eddie had killed his boy, because that was one less nigga for me to kill.

Pow!

His brain and skull matter flew out of the opened window. I'd chosen that specific desolate road for a reason. See, I'd had everything mapped out for a while. It had come to a point where I didn't see men as more than objects. Ramon was just a pawn for me to get what was due to me from Eddie, but at first, I didn't plan to kill him. Like I said though, karma was a big bitch and she was also my closest friend.

It was dark as hell and there were hardly any lights on that road I'd chosen to murder on. Getting out of the car quickly, I ran around to the passenger side and opened the door. After pulling Ramon's body out, I dragged him out as far as I could. See, it didn't matter if his body was found or not. There was no way his murder could be connected to me. His body was in the state of Florida and he was known to be involved in some shady shit. If anything, the authorities would think his lifestyle had finally caught up with his ass.

Driving off, I felt a wave of relief wash over me. Everything had gone exactly the way I'd planned without a hitch.

Chapter 17

Miami

Three months ago

A bitch was rolling in the fucking dough and life was great. Having my own shit was a whole new feeling that I wasn't used to, but I loved it. After taking the money to Dutch's lawyer, I used the 25 K he gave me and some of the profit from the coke to buy more work. Ramon had taught me everything I needed to know and with his help, I had a small crew in place. Even Sita helped move that shit.

Dutch and I stayed in touch and I even smuggled a cell phone in the prison for him. He ended up getting a lesser charge and had to do a year. That was because he'd paid for that shit. His lawyer had got almost a million dollars from him. For a minute, I thought I could be with that nigga. That was until I went to visit him, and he was hugged up with some other bitch. The only reason I knew that was because of one of the guards who kept trying to holla at me.

"Why you wastin' yo' time wit' a nigga that's in prison?" He'd asked me once when I came to visit.

Then one day I was waiting to see Dutch and he approached me.

"You're wondering why it's takin' forever for you to get in to see your man, ain't you?" He had a smirk on his face as he asked.

Before I could answer, he pulled out his cell phone and showed me a picture he'd taken of Dutch and that bitch. Without saying a word, I jumped up and stormed out of the prison pissed the fuck off. Whenever Dutch called me after that, I sent his ass to voicemail. Then I blocked his number all together. I didn't need any explanation from him. The bitch in the pictures was clearly not a relative because of the intimate way he looked at her and touched her in the picture.

"Maybe you should let him explain. Maybe she's his cousin or some shit," Sita had suggested.

At that point she and Cherrie were openly in some type of relationship. Cuz was still fucking men though. I never told her about Cherrie eating me out while I was asleep.

"I don't give a fuck either way. That bitch can have Dutch." Yeah, his family had fled to Mexico to avoid charges when he got locked up and he claimed I was all he had, but that didn't even matter to me. He didn't seem to be too damn lonely.

Over time, I got closer to Ramon. Although he and Dutch were cool, it didn't sway me. That had never stopped a nigga from getting some pussy, so why should it stop me from getting some dick? Shit, it had been a while since I had my back banged out and Ramon was there. I figured, why not? One thing led to another and after that we were literally fuck buddies.

It came to a point where I started obsessing over Eddie and Chloe again. I'd even stalk their Facebook pages and fantasize about getting my revenge. At first my mind wasn't so consumed with vengeance, but with the absence of my soul, that was all I wanted. One day, Ramon walked in the room when I was on Eddie's Facebook page. I'd discovered over time that Eddie was doing big things in the A like he said he would. Not only was he on top of Atlanta's drug trade, but he was also a party promoter. He often bragged about how he was doing it big in his statuses.

He often did live videos boasting about his money and all the shit he had. I could see that his house was laid, and he had a few nice, luxury cars. That nigga was always flossing for the book, which would be his downfall.

"What you lookin' at?" Ramon asked.

I looked back and spotted him staring down at the laptop's screen. "A potential lick," I told him.

"So, y'en satisfied with controllin' the drug game? You wanna start robbin' niggas too."

"Well, one specific nigga, yeah."

After giving him a quick run-down of what Eddie had done to me, he smirked in my direction.

"So, you wanna get yo' ex back for some shit he did five years ago?" He shook his head as he rolled a blunt.

"The way I see it, he owes me. I got a plan and I want you in on it."

His eyebrows rose as he nodded. "I'm down, but you gotta let me in on the plan."

"I was close to his sister, so I'm gonna contact her on Facebook and get more information. She's gonna be ready to brag to me about how far her brother has come. See, she's gonna think I'm still that naïve ass bitch she once knew, so she won't hold nothing back."

"A'ight. Shit, I'm down for whatever. I'm just gon' need another nigga in on this wit' me."

"Who? I ain't tryna split the money three ways."

"Don't worry ma. I'll give that nigga a cut, but it won't be an even split."

"I guess," I told him skeptically.

"Relax baby." He started massaging my shoulders. "You want that nigga dead or nah?"

"Nah, I want him to live wit' the fact that everything he worked so hard to build is gone. Just like me."

So, over the course of the next few weeks, I planned that shit to a tee. Once I got in contact with Alicia, I realized that I was right. She was ready to spill her guts about Eddie's money and coke stash.

"Yo, my bro is doin' big shit now. He's been saving up for the past few years because he just knows he's gonna get you back."

That was all I needed to hear.

Over time she revealed more, but she let me know that he didn't keep anything at his crib.

She also didn't reveal anything about where his stash house was. That meant the robbery had to be up close and personal.

So, I was already in contact with my mom who had contacted Aunt B first. We'd been talking for months and she was the perfect diversion. If I pretended that my visit to Atlanta was all about patching up my relationship with her, I'd have the perfect excuse to be there. What my mother didn't know was, I had no intentions of fucking with her like that. I hated that bitch and I always would. All I wanted from her was a reason to be in Atlanta. I'd thought of getting her ass back too, but nah. Once she realized that I wasn't dealing with her for real, that was all the get back I needed.

The plan was to make Eddie think I was not interested in him at all. Long as I threw him off, he'd have no clue that I'd set up the robbery. Conveniently, I would find a way to chill with him on my last night there. Once I had his address, I'd text it to Ramon and leave the front door unlocked, so he and his partner could slip in. The plan was fool proof since I'd be treated as a victim too. Ramon would use my life as leverage so Eddie would take him to the stash house and give up the shit.

"He'll do anything to protect me," I told Ramon. "So, you don't have to worry about him not doin' exactly what you tell him to do."

"You gon' have to give that nigga some pussy though. That way, he won't be suspicious 'cause he'll be all pussy whipped again. I know how good that shit is." He licked his lips.

That rubbed me the wrong way, because if that nigga Ramon gave a fuck about me, he wouldn't want me to fuck another nigga, not even my ex.

"I was thinkin' about almost goin' through wit' it and then makin' up an excuse not to. Then we'd fall asleep and you'd bust up in there and shit wit' your boy."

Shaking his head, there was a contemplative look on his face. "Nah ma, you gotta take it there and make that shit convincin'. You don't want him to suspect you, so fuck the shit outta that nigga. It's just fuckin'. It ain't like y'en never fucked him before."

That shit made me think about how my mother's husband profited from her fucking other men. It was slightly different, but it was the same. In a way he was pimping me out. Although the lick was my idea, he was acting like he was the one calling all the shots. That shit made me feel some type of way, but I needed him. I'd thought of doing the robbery myself, but I didn't want Eddie to know I was the culprit.

"Okay," I finally agreed, but I was looking at Ramon sideways.

Then I thought about what I was going to do to that bitch Chloe. Shit, I had something in mind.

* * *

The clinic was packed and as I walked up to the receptionist, I let her know why I was there.

"Eight thirty am appointment?" She smiled pleasantly at me as she confirmed.

"Yes."

She passed me a clip board, so I could fill out the necessary information. See, I was there for a full STD test, but I knew I was clean. A bitch had not slipped up since Rahz, so I was good. I was there in search of something else.

After I had my STD tests done, I paid the extra few hundred dollars to get my results right away. Just like I thought, everything was negative. Once I was in the waiting area again, my eyes landed on this tense looking dude. He was standing there reading something with a devastated look on his face.

Keeping my sight trained on him, I watched him leave and pull out his cell phone. There was a slight distance between us, but I could hear him loud and clear.

"Bitch, you gave me fuckin' herpes!" He thought he was talking low, but he wasn't.

As he made his way through the parking lot, I walked to my car. Not letting him out of my sight, I waited for him to end his tense call. He was standing at a car which was not too far from mine. As soon as he opened his car door, I approached him.

"Look, you gon' think I'm crazy, but hear me out."

With tears in his eyes, the handsome, mocha complexioned man looked back at me. "What do you want? I'on know you."

"You don't have to know me, but I know you pissed off right now. I also know that the meds you'll need will be expensive. I have a proposition for you that'll make a fucked up day seem a little bit better."

His face lit up with interest and I let him in on what I was scheming about. "See, it's this bitch I hate with all my heart. I want to make her life miserable. Not that I was bein' nosey, but I couldn't help but over hear your conversation."

"So, what do you want me to do and what am I gonna get out of it?"

"I want you to spark up a relationship with that bitch on line. Create a profile on one of those dating sites and then create a Facebook with a false name. Post pics of yourself though, so when you meet, she'll be down. I want you to fuck that bitch until you can't fuck no more. Make sure she's infected. If she insists on you wearing a condom, break it, take it off, I don't give a fuck. Just don't let that bitch leave without gettin' that shit. Say you're from VA or something and then meet her at Myrtle Beach in South Carolina. She loves the beach. After you fuck the bitch delete all your social media profiles. Also, make sure you don't send her any pictures of you, so you won't get in any trouble. I got ten thousand dollars up front, but I'll have ten thousand more for you when the job is done. Are you down?"

It didn't take much for me to convince him, and we shook on it.

"What's your name by the way?"

"Sean."

"It's nice meeting you Sean. I'm Xa."

"Nice meeting you too Xa."

* * *

Being that I had a key to Ramon's crib, I walked right on in without tellin him I was on my way. The thing was, I caught a snippet of a conversation that he was having on his cell phone. He didn't even know that I was there.

"Shit, she still fuckin' with Dutch. Once that nigga's out she aint' gon' fuck wit' me no more. I'm thinkin' 'bout poppin' that bitch. Shit, you'll get a half a mill and we'll be good."

He let out a sinister laugh. "Hell yeah, my nigga. Her pussy's great, but we talkin' 'bout a million dollars."

So, he wouldn't know that I heard him, I acted as if I was just walking in and slammed the door. That was when he came out of to greet me.

"Babe." He smiled and then leaned over to kiss me.

At that moment, I knew for a fact that I couldn't trust him. Doubt had crossed my mind, but until that very moment it wasn't warranted.

"Did you reup babe?" My facial expression didn't change, or show him what I knew.

"Yup, we good."

That's when I smiled and kissed him before getting undressed. Knowing that he'd want some pussy that night, I told him that I was on my period and he left me alone. The next day I went to visit Dutch for the first time in months.

* * *

"Why y'en been answering my calls?" The look on his face let me know that he was pissed.

"Don't even pull that bullshit. I know 'bout you and that bitch who's been comin' to see you."

A look of confusion came over his face. "What the fuck you talkin' 'bout?"

"I knew you'd pull that confused shit."

His stare was intense. "Talk to me ma."

I went on to explain what the CO had shown me.

"That hatin' ass mufucka. He just mad 'cause the female CO he tryna push up on wants to give me some pussy. That was my brother's shorty." As he looked around he lowered his voice. "She brought a lil' something in here for me to... sell."

"Ohhh..." Feeling dumb as hell, I tried to play it off. "Why didn't you tell me 'bout her."

"Baby, that don't matter. I'll be out in a few months and I wanna make sure yo' fine ass gon' be waitin'."

Leaving out the fact that I was fucking Ramon, I did fill him in on our plan with Eddie.

Then I told him about how I overheard that nigga planning my demise.

Dutch's face didn't change. "Go along with that shit. Once you get to Florida pop him and that nigga."

"How the fuck am I gonna kill two men by myself?"

"If you got to, turn them against each other." Something told me Dutch had an inkling about me and Ramon fucking around. "Tell Ramon that nigga tryna fuck you, or he's planning to take him out for all the money. Get Ramon to murk him. Just make sure both of 'em ain't breathin' when you get back to Miami." His voice was a whisper and couldn't be heard over the chatter in the visiting room.

Making sure that nobody was paying us any mind, I glanced around.

"Part of the reason I been callin' you, is 'cause you won't believe who just got transferred here."

"Who?"

He mouthed, "Rahz."

"What?"

"Yeah, that nigga's been here for 'bout two months."

"You got access to him?"

"He in the same damn unit as me, although he got fuckin' life."

"That's crazy."

"Tell me about it. You ain't gotta ask me to. I got that shit."

Looking around at the CO's around me, I didn't ask him any questions. He already knew all about how Rahz had ruined my fucking life. No matter what, he was willing to kill for me. I'd never taken a life at that point by my own hands. Dealing with the drug game, I'd put out a hit a few times. To do that shit myself would be a different story, but I wasn't afraid to murk a mufucka if I had to.

"Do what you gotta do baby. Fuck Ramon. I thought I could trust him enough to put you on to him, but I see that I was wrong. I'll be out soon and we gon' take over the whole fuckin' world."

So, I left knowing that I couldn't let Ramon know that I was on to his plan. His boy Jay had drove to Atlanta a day before the shit went down. Everything didn't go as planned though. I had no idea that Eddie would kill Jay. Those niggas had messed up by turning their backs on him. He was concerned about me, but once he knew I was okay, he was consumed with killing them.

So, although I wanted vindication, I didn't want anybody to die. That was until I found out that Ramon wanted to kill me. My soul was non-existent and although I was no killer, don't push me. When it came to my own existence I'd do what I had to do. Fuck anybody else. Ramon and Jay were dead because of their own greed. If only they'd gone along with the initial plan, they'd still be alive.

* * *

Miami
The Present

I'd been back in Miami for a few days, so I delivered the last ten thousand dollars to Sean being that it was confirmed that he'd done the deed. That bitch Chloe would have herpes for the rest of her life, just like I had to live with the pain she'd caused me. Finally able to sit down and chill, I noticed that Dutch was calling me from his cell phone.

"How did that shit go?" He asked.

"As planned."

"Good."

"What about that other lil' situation?" My heartbeat increased.

"Shit, I got pull in this bitch. A nigga wit' life owed me a favor and that nigga got shanked in the shower."

Yes, Rahz was dead and gone. I'd had a few calls from Eddie, Alicia and my mom. I was ignoring them and had plans to change my number soon. It was time to turn the page to a new chapter in my life.

"Thank you, Dutch, for everything."

"Yeah, but are we gon' be together when I get out?"

Not able to give him an answer straight out, I thought about it. When it came to matters of the heart, it wasn't easy for me. I'd been hurt so many times and it was probably my fault being that I put

258 | A Heartless Goon Snatched My Soul

myself out there. Eddie had shattered my ability to love and Rahz had destroyed my ability to give a fuck. My ability to sympathize and empathize had been destroyed too. At that point I didn't need a man for financial support anymore, nor did I need a man to validate me. If anything, a man was just a tool to for me to use.

I needed to bust a nut every now and then though. Now that was a must. My sex drive had faltered, but it didn't go away for good. Using my goods and getting what I wanted had become fun to me. A bitch only needed a man for an occasional orgasm, or to commit a murder. Shit, I had my own money.

Would I really wait for Dutch? Who knew? Maybe one day I'd be able to love again. Right now, my bank was bigger than any dick I'd ever seen, and the world was in the palm of my hands.

"We'll see Dutch," was my simple response.

My first love had stolen my heart, and a heartless goon had snatched my soul, but I was still alive. Everybody who wronged me had got theirs back ten-fold. Now, it was my time to live and my mission was to do that shit to the fullest on my own damn terms.

Thank you so much for reading. I hope you enjoyed and I am grateful for your support!!!

-**Nika Michelle**

More books by Nika Michelle

http://amzn.to/2AwWdks

About the Author

Nika Michelle is originally from NC and currently resides in Atlanta, GA. Her love for books started at a very young age and inspired her passion for writing. Blessed with a vivid imagination, she would share her short stories with her classmates in middle and high school. In 2002 she graduated from Fayetteville State University with a BA in Communications and English/Literature. During her time in college she completed her first novel "Forbidden Fruit", an urban tale that spins a web of love, lust and greed. Her other titles include Forbidden Fruit 2: A New Seed, Forbidden Fruit 3: The Juice, Forbidden Fruit 4: The Last Drop, Forbidden Fruit 5: The Final Taste, Forbidden Fruit 6, Black Butterfly, Black Onyx: The Sequel to Black Butterfly, Black Magic: Book 3 of the Black Butterfly Series, Black Lace: Book 4 of the Black Butterfly Series, Zero Degrees 1, 2 and 3 (collaboration with Leo Sullivan), The Nookie Ain't Free, The Nookie Still Ain't Free, The Empress, That "D" On the Side, Bout That Life: Diablo's Story (A Forbidden Fruit Prequel) and Love In the A (A Forbidden Fruit Spin Off). Love In The A 2: Thicker Than Blood, Love In The A 3: Bad Blood and Love In the A 4: Flesh and Blood, The Plug's Daughter, The Plug's Daughter 2: It's Love and War, The Reunion: A Forbidden Fruit Story, The Reunion: A Forbidden Fruit Story 2, A Pimp In Pumps, In

Love With a Rude Boy: A Top Shotta's Love Story (with Raquel Williams), Pistol's Grip (An Urban Love Tale), Pistol's Grip 2 (An Urban Love Tale), Pistol's Grip 3 (An Urban Love Tale), Crazy In Love: A Twisted Urban Romance 1 & 2, and Cheating On The Plug: A Risky Love Affair.

91753323R00146

Made in the USA
Middletown, DE
02 October 2018